The Last

Hour

Paul A. Tardo

Scripture references are taken from THE INTERLINEAR GREEK-ENGLISH NEW TESATMENT by Alfred Marshall D.Litt. Published by Zondervan Publishing House   First printing copyright© 1975 and second printing copyright© 1976

THE INTERLINEAR GREEK-ENGLISH NEW TESATMENT by George Ricker Berry Published by Zondervan Publishing House   25th printing copyright ©1981

The King James Version with the archaic words like ye and thee changed to more modern ones.

ISBN: 978-1-60383-054-6

Published by:
Holy Fire Publishing
Unit 116
1525-D Old Trolley Rd.
Summerville, SC 29485

www.ChristianPublish.com

Cover Design: Jay Cookingham

Printed in the United States of America and the United Kingdom

Dedication

This book can be dedicated to no one else but Jesus Himself. It is His for only He can share the depth of His sufferings and He truly is worthy of our love for the price He paid to bring us to Himself.

Table Of Contents

INTRODUCTION

Throughout all the ages, throughout all time, throughout all the acts of mankind, in all the plays, in all the movies, in all the television, and in all the drama that has ever played out before us, nowhere and at no time has anyone uttered a more tragic, moving, overwhelming, and least understood set of words than what Jesus said in the last moments of the last hours of His crucifixion. The words, "My God, My God, why have You forsaken Me?" echo through all time as the most important words we will ever hear and the least comprehended.

Why? What brought our Lord to this cry? What does it mean to us today? How can we understand the words unless we know what Jesus was thinking in giving them? How can we fully apply the cross to our lives unless we know the answers as to what brought Him to make such a cry? Jesus was completely confident as to who He was despite the brutal torture He endured before they placed Him on the cross. Then, after they raised Him up on the wood, did He not ask His heavenly Father to forgive the ones who did not know what they were doing? Again, three hours after the horrors of the death of the cross, He confidently told a thief that in the same day they were dying, he would be with Him in Paradise. What changed? All that man could do to Him did nothing to give us the slightest hint of any question like as the one He asked after the last hours of His time on the cross.

Many have seen a small part of the torture of the Jews and the Romans in Mel Gibson's movie about the passion of Christ. Multitudes were moved to tears and even a change of lifestyle just for seeing the torture man put on our Lord. What Mel Gibson showed was only part of the sufferings of Christ. I pray Jesus would share His sufferings of His last hours with you through this book and His Holy Spirit.

CHAPTER ONE

THE HEART OF OUR HEAVENLY FATHER IN CHRIST'S DEATH

God put a multitude of prophecies of Christ coming and the cross to which He destined Him. To predict the detail we find in the written word of Jesus and His death so many years before the event would be impossible except the living God should have inspired the prophecies. Jesus fulfilled them all. In this book, I will show even more that you might find fellowship with Jesus and the Father's sufferings. Starting with the Father, I pray you can have a glimpse into His heart in this matter of Jesus needing to go to the cross for us.

The most famous scripture of the Bible is held up in nationally televised sports events and quoted to them who do not know Jesus or what He did for them. Fans at football games hold up signs with the scripture boldly proclaiming the hope of salvation for all mankind. We quote it to witness of Jesus as our Savior. John 3:16 is that verse and it says, "For God so loved the world, that He gave His only begotten Son, that whosoever believes in Him should not perish, but have everlasting life." The decision maker in this verse is God. It is the Father of our Lord Jesus Christ. However, believing in God, according to these words of Jesus will never be enough to keep anyone from eternally perishing. Doing works for the great God who is the Father of Jesus Christ will not save a soul from eternal darkness and the fires of it. The heavenly Father has made believing in Jesus Christ the only way to salvation. Jesus has told us this for it is what the Father told Him.

In the words of this most famous of scriptures, we see the depths of our heavenly Father's being. He loved us so much that He gave us Jesus Christ. When Jesus asked if any way other than the cross could save us, John 3:16 must have come back to His thoughts. Therefore, He must go to the cross. He is the only hope to bring any to the eternal life our heavenly Father wants to give us.

Let us wonder just what our heavenly Father thought as He sent Jesus to the cross. In a prophetic story of King David, we see the Father's thoughts. In one tragic moment in David's history, God reveals the great depth of emotion our heavenly Father had over the matter. In the analogy of the natural, we can peer into the spiritual. I pray your soul can look deeply into the heart of the Father and see His pain in the matter of seeing His Son being the only way to eternal life for anyone.

Due to the great sin of David, the peace of his house became a place of struggle. His firstborn son, Absalom, rose up against him. In the time of battle, Absalom became caught in a great oak tree. II Samuel 18:9 says, "His head caught hold of the oak, and he was taken up between heaven and earth." Just like Jesus hung between heaven and earth on the cross for taking on the sins of the whole world, so did hang the firstborn son of David. There, hanging on the tree did they kill Absalom and there hanging on the tree did Jesus die.

When David heard the news of his son's death, II Samuel 18:33 tells of what he did and said. "And the king was much moved, and went up to the chamber above the gate, and wept: and as he went, thus he said, O my son Absalom! Would God I had died for You, O Absalom, my son, my son!" Within the darkness of this analogy, the great light of understanding rests. If it were possible, our heavenly Father would have given His life for Jesus. If it were possible, He would have died rather than Him. If any other way existed to save us, even the Father giving His life, it would have been done. Even though we yet may not fully understand the love and righteousness of it all, we can at the least know Jesus' death on the cross was the only way to bring salvation and healing to us. The pain and sorrow of our heavenly Father cannot be expressed fully in this little analogy. We can get a small glimpse of His perfect love for Jesus and for us in letting His Son be raised between heaven and earth to die for our sins. Should not our souls bow to the earth in some measure of loving understanding?

Who cannot see the heartbreak of a father who suffers the pain of the death of a son and not weep with Him? When I was twenty, John lost his son of sixteen years in a swimming accident. Due to the car problems of my ride to the funeral, we missed it and his burial. However, at the house, I saw John for the first time since the death of his son. His hair had a lot of newly formed gray running through it and his face showed the sorrow of the hour. Though very sad about his son's death, I was moved to tears in seeing John's countenance. Just so, let us begin to understand how much sorrow Jesus' last day caused our heavenly Father.

There is more. We have a little more light to shine upon our seeing Jesus, the Son of God born of a virgin, coming to the earth in this analogy of Absalom. A time earlier, before David's firstborn's death on the tree, Absalom was separated from the comforts and position of the high places of David's family for three years. During that separation, "David mourned for his son every day." The Lord of glory, the Son of God in the heavens became a man. The humility of it, the wonder of it still brings awe to our understanding. What we know is too much to fully take in when we put our thoughts to it. However, our heavenly Father also suffered in the change. There was sadness and a missing of their perfect union they had in heaven. Even so, even though our heavenly Father mournfully missed Jesus being one with Him as before, for us, for you and me, He pressed through to even see His Son die.

I pray this gives all a greater insight of the great love our heavenly Father has for us. It is even as Jesus' High Priestly prayer in John 17 reveals. After praying for the disciples Jesus says, "Neither pray I for these alone, but for them also which shall believe on Me through their word; that they all may be one; as You, Father are in Me, and I in You, that they also may be one in us: that the world may believe that You have sent Me. And the glory which You have given Me I have given them; that they may be one, even as we are one: I in them, and You in Me, that they may be made perfect in one; and that the world may know that you have sent Me, and have loved them, as You have loved Me." O, do you see it?

There is absolutely no way our heavenly Father would have allowed Jesus to come and send Him to die for us if He did not love us as He loves Him. I pray you can see just how much you are loved either as one who will repent of your sins and give your life to Jesus to save or as one already raised in newness of life in Christ Jesus our Lord. Whatever you do, you must know Jesus came and died because it was the only way to bring eternal life to us.

If you have asked Jesus to forgive and save you, I pray reading this book will bring you closer to the unity He wants us to have with Him and our heavenly Father.

If you have not given your life to Jesus or have taken some part of it back, I pray you would fellowship with Jesus in this book unto fulfilling His prayer of unity with you. O, will you not give all your love to God through Jesus as He has given all His love to you?

CHAPTER TWO

SINGULAR OR PLURAL

"He was wounded for our transgressions, He was bruised for our iniquities: the chastisement of our peace was upon Him; and with His stripes we are healed."

Isaiah 53:5

Mel Gibson's movie about the passion of our Lord Jesus started with this verse. No matter what you think of Mr. Gibson or his movie, anyone that has seen his portrayal of Christ's crucifixion would have a greater visible view of some of the terrible physical sufferings Jesus faced in that day of the Lord. In an interview, Mr. Gibson said they could not show all the sufferings Jesus went through. He said it would have been too much. He was right. There were beatings by a battalion of soldiers after the scourging which left him unrecognizable. There can be no doubt of the fulfillment of Isaiah 52:14 which shows Jesus was tortured and disfigured beyond any man before Him or after.

The stripes the Romans gave our Lord Jesus only represent a small part of His sufferings. Mr. Gibson made the stripes the worst of it. The worst came after the stripes. We might wonder. If the stripes were all it took to bring our healing, why did Jesus need to continue suffering? Why did our heavenly Father allow Jesus to go through the terrible torture of the Roman battalion? In their persecution after the scourging, the Romans had beaten and marred Jesus so much that when it came time to carry His physical cross, he could not carry it. So, if His stripes alone were enough to bring about our healing, why did our heavenly Father let Jesus go on to the cross?

Other translations seem to answer that question. When Peter quotes Isaiah 53:5, the King James Version states that we are healed by His stripes, but other translations tell us Peter says we are healed by His wounds. We now could account for all the wounds including the nails in Jesus' hands and feet. As we accept all the wounds our Lord received, including them given to Him on the cross, we might say all that the Israelites and the Romans did to Jesus brought our healing.

We might say that, but that is not the whole truth. A strange thing has happened in this passage about what brought our healing. The Cambridge reference for the King James states that the word "Stripes" literally means a singular "Bruise." The Hebrew English Old Testament and The Septuagint both show that the word "Stripes" means literally a singular "Bruise." Let us also note that Peter's quotation of Isaiah 53:5 is in the singular as well.

Nestle and Marshall's The Interlinear Greek and English New Testament literally quotes I Peter 2:24. They say Peter said, "Who the sins of us Himself carried up in the body of Him onto the tree, in order

16

that to sins dying to righteousness we might live; of whom by the bruise ye were cured." The Interlinear Greek and English New Testament by George Berry translates this passage by Peter this way. "By whose bruise ye were healed." Thus, the experts in Greek know the Greek word for stripes or wounds is not plural, but one singular wound.

What did Isaiah and Peter mean by the "Bruise?" Our translators brought us to believe and teach the plural. The stripes or wounds are the words that we understood brought our healing. Are we now to find that the translators interpreted the word rather than translated it? Isaiah and Peter wrote of a singular bruise. According to the original language, a singular bruise brings us healing.

The thinking of the ones who made this singular word to become translated to be plural is simple. The experts on Hebrew decided that they should translate the singular word "Bruise" in the plural on the principle of "Non conventional collectives." Bruce Waltke and M. O'Conner in their book Biblical Hebrew Syntax said, "Non conventional collectives are words that are often represented by the plural but for contextual reasons may be represented by a collective." A collective word is a word that is either singular or plural. Mainly they occur in natural things like seed, fruit, and fish. However, when the translators came to the singular bruise in the book of Isaiah, they made it plural on the principle of non-conventional collectives. The translators saw the many wounds of the Lord and decided the word was plural.

We must recognize that Peter destroys any such argument of the translators of the Old Testament. He knew the Hebrew. He knew that the word was singular. He saw all the wounds our Lord took. Yet, he made it singular too. If non-conventional collectives applied to the bruise, then Peter would have made the Greek word plural. This he did not do. Peter followed the original Hebrew in his quotation. He made the bruise singular as seen in his Greek letters.

Kenneth Wuest in his translation wrote of I Peter 2:24. He tried to explain the way Peter wrote of the singular bruise by saying, "The word stripe is in the singular here; a picture of our Lord's back after the scourging, one mass of raw, quivering flesh with no skin remaining, trickling with blood." It is hard to read those words and immediately press forward in our understanding, but there is so much more to know.

Mr. Wuest did not fall upon the contextual collective of the Hebrew as the excuse to make the stripe plural. No, he could not. He was translating from the Greek. The picture that he saw of the beaten Christ brought him to interpret, but he rightly did say it was a singular stripe. In defense of all, without revelation of what bruise brought our healing, the interpretation is understandable.

When Isaiah wrote his now famous verse about what brought our healing, he heard from God to use the word bruise in the singular form. He was not looking at Jesus on the cross. He had no idea what the bruise meant or what manner the Lamb of God should die. He only knew to say what God told him to say. He knew nothing of non-standard collectives. He only knew to give the words as God gave them to him.

Take into consideration the Septuagint. It was the Greek translation of the Hebrew by the natural Israelites for them who knew Greek but not Hebrew. They too had no idea of just what would bring our healing. Therefore, the Greek version of Isaiah 53:5 translates it the way it was written making our healing to come from one singular "Bruise."

Peter read Isaiah in the original Hebrew. Perhaps he read the Septuagint as well. He was very familiar with Isaiah 53. I imagine he recited that famous chapter more than once in witnessing to his fellow countrymen. He certainly knew it well enough to put it in his first letter. Peter also was very familiar with exactly what our Lord Jesus suffered on the cross. Now I ask you. When he was about to quote Isaiah 53:5 for his letter, why did he choose to make the stripe Jesus took to bring about our healing singular? After all, Peter would have seen the many stripes and bruises given to Jesus in His suffering like as is the argument of our modern day translators. Surely, of all the ones to quote Isaiah 53:5, he would have understood the principle of "Non standard collectives." Thus, according to the thinking of the translators and theologians he should have made it plural. Then, we perfectly would understand all the wounds Jesus suffered were what brought our healing. Yet, Peter did not do that. He made the bruise that brought our healing singular.

Why? Why would Peter ignore all the stripes and bruises? Why would he have looked upon the word and left it singular? He saw the cross and he saw Isaiah 53:5. He could have used the same explanation all the translators and theologians used to make the bruise plural. They all, even as one voice changed it to the plural stripes, but Peter did not follow their logic. Did Peter know something about the bruise that the many translators and theologians did not?

We have no explanation other than that he must have known more. Peter saw the bruise that brought our healing. He did not need to interpret Isaiah 53:5. Rather, he only needed to accurately quote him in this matter.

With respect for the men who know the languages, the word "Stripes" is wrong. Only one bruise brought our healing. Peter knew that the word was singular and he knew what the bruise was. Otherwise, he would have translated it in the plural and all the translators would not have needed to explain away why Peter did that. Truly, for us to say that it was a collective is wrong. Peter did not follow that logic and neither should we.

Even so, many will have a very difficult time changing in this matter. If you should wish to continue with the translators view, it is understandable. You can see that the one singular bruise could not have come without all that happened to Jesus before it. All the wounds fit together as part of the process that brought the fulfillment of the bruise that brings our healing. Thus, you can say the scourging the Romans gave Jesus precluded the bruise that brought our healing. We also can say the wounds of the nails came in sequence to what brought our healing. However, it is imperative to our spiritual growth to know that these wounds lead to the one singular bruise that Isaiah wrote of and Peter must have seen.

Let us ask why God had Isaiah write of the singular bruise that would bring our healing. Let us ask just what stripe or bruise brought our healing? What did Peter know that we need to understand and why is it so important to us anyway?

It is important because, "By His bruise we were healed." The word healed also is translated made whole. We are made whole by one particular wound. If our healing became a result of the one bruise, we must know what it is for it to have its greatest power to heal us. Thus, we can begin to understand the great depth of Christ's sufferings and the power to heal it brings us.

It is important so that Jesus can make us whole and wholly healed by knowing just what this bruise was. I know it was so with me and I believe if you understand this part of Jesus' sacrifice on the cross, it will become extremely important to you. Like Colossians 1:9-10 says. Understanding the bruise will bring the healing of it unto a worthier walk with Jesus.

CHAPTER THREE

THE BRUISE

We all could easily follow the theology of the translators and not enter the depth of this message. We could continue to sing the song that says we will never know how much it cost to see our sins upon the cross. Or, we can bow our selves to God and desire to know more of the cost to the heart and soul of our Lord and Savior, Jesus Christ in this time of the cross. Indeed, as we press to know Jesus in this, we can have the great privilege of fellowshipping in His sufferings of the cross as well. I know of no greater suffering Christ knew then this time of the cross. To them that press to win Christ, sharing in His sufferings will be a great part of our call to win Him.

Some prefer not to know the depth of Christ's sacrifice. Thus, they would not have any conviction for living a less than a wholehearted dedication and purposed life for Christ. I pray seeing just how much it cost Jesus to heal us will bring all to be more wholeheartedly purposed to serve Jesus alone.

So, what singular wound could bring our healing and make us whole? To learn, I first ask you to take of the bread and wine of Christ's sacrifice and remember, looking upon our suffering Lord. He faced the Jewish mockery of a trial and their persecution. He survived the Roman scourging and their beatings even though they made Him unrecognizable. He was so beaten beyond recognition that the Romans made another carry the wood to Calvary. Then the nails fastened Him securely to His fate. Finally, they lifted Him up to face all that would torment Him.

After that, Luke tells us He said, "Father, forgive them; for they know not what they do." Can you hear the confidence in His voice? Do you see the suffering Son of God to be uncertain of who He was or what He was doing? All that man did to Jesus could not break Him or make Him question the events of His mission. Rather, according to Matthew 5:44-45, He proved His Sonship by praying for them who bitterly persecuted Him. Jesus was just as strong and certain of His place as God's Son and what He was doing as when the angel came to strengthen Him in Gethsemane.

Then, for three hours Jesus said nothing. He suffered all the pain of the cross, but still said nothing. No matter what taunt the crowd hit him with, He was silent even as a lamb being sheared.

Finally, the thief spoke. For three hours he watched Jesus take the abuse without any verbal defense or reprisal. He saw a man beaten beyond recognition. He heard Him ask forgiveness for the ones that did not know what they were doing. He heard Jesus speak intimately to God as His Father. Then, after three hours, he asked Jesus to remember him when He comes into His kingdom. Jesus answered Him with the same confidence and authority that He had when He spoke to His Father saying, "Verily I say unto you, Today you shall be with Me in paradise."

Again, after the first three hours on the cross, Jesus was as steady and sure of His place and what He was doing as when He started. Then something happened after the thief heard of his salvation from hell. Immediately after Jesus spoke to the thief, the sky filled with darkness. Jesus looked down to man during the first three hours. He looked for one that had faith. After the words of faith came from the thief, Jesus stopped looking down to man and began looking up to His Father's dwelling place. We know this to be true for Matthew, Mark, and Luke show us His Father coming down from heaven. The three gospels reveal our heavenly Father centering Himself at the cross of Christ. We know this for they all said, "From the sixth hour there was darkness over all the land unto the ninth hour."

You might think, "These gospels record darkness covering the land. Where do you find the Father coming down to the scene of the cross?" Dear friend, behind that darkness dwelled the Father.

Darkness, thick dark clouds of the sky came over the land. Darkness came down and hovered around the dying Christ. Behind that darkness, hidden from the view of all, dwelled the great brightness of our heavenly Father. Look into the following scriptures and you will see the Father coming so close that Jesus almost could touch Him. Imagine these verses from God's word. See them with the men of Old Testament that wrote them. See how they reveal God's dwelling place and greatly wonder with me. Wonder as to knowing Jesus saw His Father's dwelling place and would have reached up to touch Him except they nailed His hands securely to the crossbeam.

Of all the men and women of the Old Testament, none of their experiences with the glory and power of God can be compared to what Moses knew. Many times Israel saw Moses talking to God. They watched him go to where God was and share of the needs of the people. One time as recorded in Exodus 20:21, we see the scene. The nation of Israel kept their distance while Moses went to where God was. Read just where God was and marvel as you compare it to the darkness that hovered over the cross the last three hours of Christ's life as our sacrifice. "And the people stood afar off, and Moses drew near unto the thick darkness where God was."

Moses drew near to the thick darkness where God was. Later, as seen in Deuteronomy 5:22-23, Moses was telling the people of the words God spoke and wrote on the tables of stone. Again we see the darkness as part of God's dwelling. Moses said, "These words the Lord spoke unto all your assembly in the mount out of the midst of the fire, of the cloud, and the thick darkness, with a great voice: and He added no more. And He wrote them in the tables of stone, and delivered them unto me. And it came to pass, when ye heard the voice out of the midst of the darkness . . .." Can you picture Moses hearing from God out of the thick darkness? There stood Moses next to the thick darkness, the thick clouds that hid the great light and glory of God from view so that none would die from its intensity. Out of the midst of it came the voice of God that scared the rest of Israel so much that they told Moses to talk to God for them. Now, do you see this same darkness drawing close to Jesus? Imagine the heart of Christ seeing it!

Let us turn to Solomon. In all his wisdom and understanding, he spoke his greatest understanding in I Kings 8:12. The Bible repeats the words in II Chronicles 6:1. Whenever God repeats Himself, we know He places greater importance upon the words. Solomon had no idea of the connection to the cross and the bruise his words had. However, as we go forward, I believe you will see these words of his as his greatest ones. "Then spoke Solomon, The Lord said that He would dwell in the thick darkness." Look now upon our suffering Savior. The shade of the thick clouds started to cover Him. What thoughts must have come to Him?

A psalmist wrote. We have not his name. Yet, in a high moment of his life, the Holy Spirit opened his eyes and he put Psalm 97 together. Within that Psalm, we have verse two. The psalmist saw and said, "Clouds and darkness are round about Him: righteousness and judgment are the habitation of His throne." Imagine the psalmist being carried into the heavens to see God's dwelling place. He senses and recognizes the purity, holiness, righteousness, and judgment that establish His throne. Most of all and especially for our understanding, he sees the clouds that surround God. Thus, the psalmist could write what he saw. He saw the thick darkness. He saw the clouds. Do you see them too?

Now, look on the last three hours of Jesus' life. Look closely at the thick darkness that surrounded the land, even the whole earth according to Luke and historical data. Look at those black clouds that surrounded the awesome presence of the Father. They hid the presence of God from the view of all. The great God of heaven and earth, the Father of our Lord Jesus Christ, hid His great presence behind that darkness that covered the land. The all powerful God, who in all eternity knew oneness with His Son, now watched completely separated from Him. The Father watched and waited ever so close. He watched and waited for the culmination of the plan of the ages.

O the pain of it! Any good father who helplessly sees his son ravished from some terrible disease is moved to great sorrow and grief. Surely, he immediately will give his son the medicine needed to take away the disease. Yet, our heavenly Father, perfect as He is and knowing great pain in seeing the suffering of His only begotten Son, did nothing. He only watched. He held deliverance from Him. Yes, any good Father who has the power to free his son from undeserved trouble will do it. Our Father, the God of all, did nothing but watch. God drew so close that all there could see His dwelling place and yet, He did nothing. Can you imagine it?

Only one person knew what was happening. Yes, just one man saw those clouds and knew who dwelled behind them. Jesus looked at the darkness and saw His redemption drawing very close. All others were completely blind to just who dwelled behind those dark clouds.

What thoughts of hope moved into Jesus' heart at the first sight of that darkness? Thoughts of seeing the unbearable pain end surely must have encouraged Jesus' heart and soul. Yes, Jesus knew though no other did. Jesus now looked upward into those clouds expecting soon to see His redemption. Yet, it did not come.

Are there any words to describe the terrible pain felt in the next three hours that passed? How would you feel? What thoughts would pass through you in similar circumstances?

Suppose some radical group kidnapped you. Without any just cause, they tortured you and set you on a cross to die. Then your natural father came on the scene with untold numbers in his army. Well able to free you from your suffering, your father then just watches. Close enough to touch you; your father does nothing for the first minutes after his arrival. He does not even say hello. Then an hour later he still just watched. Two hours go by and the pain has increased horribly in this most terrible of deaths. Each second offers only great pain and no relief. By the time the third hour had come, would you say something to your father? What words would you say? How long could you wait before you spoke?

I tell you the truth. All the suffering man put upon Christ cannot compare to Jesus seeing His Father so close and yet doing nothing. Up to the moment the darkness hovered over Christ, Jesus was confident of His mission being fulfilled. At the end of three hours of silence from those clouds, He shouted His awesome cry. It came in the last hour.

Look at our suffering Savior now seeing the thick darkness where the Father dwelled. Look deep into Jesus' eyes as His soul hoped for His deliverance. Look at the first few minutes after the darkness drew near. Jesus looked up and saw His Father's dwelling place. If you can imagine it, you will see Jesus begin to hope the separation between Him and His Father would quickly end.

Jesus saw His redemption hidden behind those thick clouds. For three hours, Jesus stared into that darkness. He knew, saw, and felt the clouds' presence. His Father was so close; yet, He did nothing. What thoughts must Jesus have had as the last hours passed?

Friend, witness your suffering Savior struggling to continue. See Him looking up for deliverance without any coming. Gaze upon Jesus as He felt the pain of struggling to breathe on the cross with all His other wounds and seeing His Father's dwelling place. Can we ever find words to describe it?

Jesus said nothing for those last three hours. In all His physical pain, He also faced carrying the sins of the world, my sins and yours. He received the death we all deserved. He knew the darkness of separation from the Father. He looked and only a few feet away saw the thick clouds that hid His Father from view. Yet, He was separated from Him. Yet, He had not the communion He so longed to enter into again.

God moved ever so close and did absolutely nothing for three hours. These three hours of silence surpassed anything that Jesus' heart knew up to this point. These three hours of the Father being so close and doing nothing must have struck a deep blow to Jesus' inner being. Indeed, the pain of His Father's silence must have crushed Jesus. Isaiah 53 says, "He had done no violence, neither was any deceit in His mouth. Yet, it pleased the Father to bruise Him . . . and with His bruise we are healed." The Hebrew word for bruise in the first part of the quote means, "Crush." It pleased the Lord to crush Him. The Father crushed Jesus by coming so close and doing nothing. It pleased the Father to crush Jesus for you and me. It pleased Him for our sakes.

All that the Romans did had no effect upon Jesus' Sonship. He spoke to His Father as confidently at the beginning of His time on the cross as He did in all the days before the last hours. Yet, at the end of the three hours of darkness, He was so crushed by His Father being so close and doing nothing, that He cried out to His God rather than calling upon the intimate realm of father and son. The Father struck the bruise that crushed our Lord Jesus and what a mighty blow it was.

Imagine yourself chained and tortured while, just a few feet away, your father with an army so large it cannot be counted, just watches saying and doing nothing. Yes, imagine it and wonder with me how our Lord could have so perfectly waited for three hours before saying anything.

Each of us, who have known the great joy and peace in our union with God, also knows the pain of separation caused by sin. Except the heart harden, whenever we should fall short in some sin, we would feel an agonizing wound because that sin brought the death of separation between our God and us. Remember the pain you felt in the early days of your walk with Jesus when you fell short in some sin. Well, Jesus was one with the Father for all eternity past until this time of the cross. There He took the separation sin causes between God and man for us. There He knew the magnified pain of all the sins of the world.

He took our punishment for sin. We can know the eternal separation of Hell and the Burning Lake of Fire will be of the same sort of suffering Jesus knew on the cross. If you witness to the lost and tell them of hell, get them to look at Jesus on the cross. They will gain some idea of the pain they will know. Truly, Jesus took our eternal punishment.

Our heavenly Father came close. Jesus longed for reunion and deliverance. He looked up into the dwelling place of His Father for a sign that it would soon come. Yet, His Father did nothing. Some time after the arrival of His Father, Jesus must have begun to wonder, "What is He waiting for?

These last three hours of pain in His body and in the spirit far surpassed anything that He had suffered up to this point. We know this to be true because of what Jesus cried out at the end of those three hours of looking into the thick dark clouds. Looking and waiting, looking and waiting, looking and waiting, until He wondered if He would die without being reunited with His Father for some reason He did not know.

Jesus felt death surround Him. He knew the cords of death were about to take Him. Yet, He and His Father were still separated. He had no answer as to why. He did not know the reason He was about to die still separated from His Father. Did not the Lamb of God go through the sacrifice perfectly? Did not the Lamb of God give Himself perfectly for us? He took our sins and death so perfectly. Yet, there He was. His body was telling Him He was about to die and His Father still did nothing. What was He waiting for and why was it so?

The darkness came and after three hours, Jesus cried with a loud voice, "Eli, Eli, lama sabach-thani? That is to say, My God, My God, why have you forsaken Me?" He did not understand why He was about to physically die without His Father uniting to Him again. His Father's dwelling place was only a few feet away and He did nothing. What a blow this must have been to Jesus?

Why did the Father wait those three hours? He could have taken Jesus after the first moments of His arrival behind the thick darkness. Surely, He wanted to regain His union with Jesus as much as Jesus wanted it with Him. Why was this one specific blow of drawing so close and doing nothing needed to bring about our healing? What purpose was there for our heavenly Father to strike this blow of doing nothing in such close proximity?

Of all the stripes to hit Jesus, none compared to this. As Jesus walked through Israel, He overcame every trial, every test, and every temptation. All of it came from man, nature, and the devil. Then came the suffering of the scourging, beatings, and the cross. Still, Jesus stood strong in His purpose and place. His voice echoed the great confidence of His knowing exactly why all was happening. Up to this time, the Father never struck Him. This blow of drawing so close and doing nothing bruised Jesus in such a way as to bring our healing. Even as the scriptures say by His bruise we are healed. Yet, we must ask, "Why?" Why did the Father need to strike this one singular blow? Were not all the stripes given Him by man and the devil enough to bring our healing? Why did the Father need to strike this most powerful of blows? Are we to know this bruise brought our healing?

CHAPTER FOUR

PSALM 51:17

Psalm 51:17 states that, "The sacrifices of God are a broken spirit: a broken and a contrite heart You will not despise." The greatest sacrifice of God, to be acceptable and perfected, needed a broken heart and spirit. Without them broken, a perfect sacrifice could not exist. Jesus' sacrifice was perfected through His suffering. The blow to cause the bruise by which we were to be healed truly must be powerful enough to have broken open Jesus' spirit. All that man did had no effect upon Jesus' spirit. Only our heavenly Father had the power to strike such a blow as to break it open.

Proverbs 15:13 tells us the way to a broken spirit. "By sorrow of the heart the spirit is broken." I ask you. How much more sorrow could a heart feel than what Jesus knew on the cross and by the blow of His Father being so close and doing nothing to deliver Him? Have you not known this in a much smaller measure? You have prayed hard upon a need so pressing that your prayers were laced with much travail of heart and soul. Yet, silence was all that came in return. The trial continued without relief. Did not this bring so much sorrow that you thought even your spirit would break. Then, it did. Indeed, has not God's silence done just that? If what was in your spirit was some defilement (II Cor. 7:1), then it would flow out into all that you thought, felt, and did. The hope of our Lord in this for those with a defiled spirit is to show

35

just what dwelled in us and of our great need to cleanse it. However, with Jesus, there was no deceit in Him. There was no defilement in His heart or spirit. Still, according to the written word of God, a sacrifice of God must have a broken heart and spirit.

Therefore, the blow of silence struck hard upon our Lord's inner being. It brought a sorrow that broke His heart. His sorrow brought such a breaking that it finally broke His spirit as well. Then the scripture was fulfilled. Then the sacrifice for you and I was complete. The sacrifice of a broken spirit perfected Jesus.

His Spirit had to be broken for the sacrifice to be complete. His Spirit must have all its' contents poured out for an acceptable sacrifice. Yes, truly the sacrifice of the cross, to be a sacrifice of God, had to have a broken spirit. Can you see Jesus' cry asking why He was forsaken mark the very moment His spirit was broken? Can you see the pure faith that dwelled in Him in His cry seeking a reason why He was forsaken?

O, do you see it? Isaiah said it pleased the Father to crush Him. The crushing blow came by our heavenly Father coming so close and doing nothing. That bruise broke Christ's Spirit. Out came all that was within it. Can you see the moment when Jesus felt the cords of death choking His life out of Him? The sorrow of heart of not knowing why He and the Father were not yet one came. In the test of despair and desperation, He cried out to His God knowing His belief in Him will open the way to the answer. Like Adam, if He failed in some area and lost His intimate relationship as Son, then God would still be His God. He still could ask

Him why He was forsaken. He could ask His God why He was not reunited with Him. He could ask Him in perfect faith.

Only the purest of faith dwelled in Christ. That faith poured out of His broken spirit. Jesus was seeking His God to know why He was about to die without them being reunited. Hebrews 11:6 tells us faith is believing God is and that He is a rewarder of them that seek Him. When death was about to strangle Jesus with the Father still doing nothing, our Lord's spirit broke. The purest of faith poured out and opened the way for all to receive the whole of the sacrifice of God. Then, after the cry, our heavenly Father answered Him immediately. I must wait to show this by the scriptures until later. For now, we must see ourselves in Christ's sacrifice.

CHAPTER FIVE

FIRST JESUS AND THEN US

The sacrifices of God is a plural statement. It started with Jesus and now has come to us. "The sacrifices of God are a broken spirit: a broken and a contrite heart, O God, You will not despise." God calls us to be part of the sacrifice of Christ. As the body has many parts yet is one body, just so is the sacrifice of Christ on Calvary. It is one sacrifice; yet, it only will be seen in the many parts of Jesus' Body. May the grace of Jesus Christ, bring us all to become the sacrifices of God.

Jesus took the pain, the suffering, and the separation as the Lamb of God, so that we who would believe in His sacrifice on the cross would not have to know it. God uses circumstances and things to bring us to understand, to correct, to guide, and to bring us closer to Him.

Even so, He will never intend them to be the source of our broken spirit and heart unless sin and defilement of spirit is involved. The hardness, troubles, and tribulations of life can break our hearts, even our spirits if sin is their cause. They can come upon us with such force that we are crushed. For the one that sin so dominates them who yet would desire to be one with Christ, the trials reveal their sins and a small part of the punishment for them. Sin brought on the crushing of Jesus so that we could be healed. If sin has dominion over us, and we are not reprobate, the crushing bruises that God sends are meant to break our hearts and spirits before Him. Like a little child needing correcting punishment, it will come. It is so because as many as Jesus loves, He rebukes and chastens (Rev. 3:19).

However, them who truly are healed by Christ's bruise will not know the troubles of life to come to break them. Rather, the much tribulations of life will come to bring them into the kingdom of God.

For the ones who were healed by the bruise, like the Apostle Paul, the situations of life are meant to bring them into the kingdom. Just like the Apostle Paul said, "We must through much tribulation enter the kingdom of God." All the tests and troubles that come our way should only be to bring us to come into the kingdom of heaven if we are healed by His bruise. Romans 14:17 says the kingdom of God is righteousness, peace, and joy in the Holy Spirit. Therefore, all that comes our way should bring us to draw closer to Jesus and the kingdom in the Holy Spirit if we were healed by His bruise. If we are not yet healed, even made whole by the bruise of Christ, then the troubles come to break open our hearts and spirits to expose the defilements in them so we can come to the Godly sorrow needed to see them cleansed and healed forever.

We are to have Godly sorrow if we fail and sin. When sin enters, we have a choice. We choose between having Godly sorrow or the worldly kind. The Apostle Paul says worldly sorrow works death. Surely, if we have truly repented of our sins and taken Jesus as our

Savior, we would not want to just have worldly sorrow for sin. Why would any who have tasted of the age to come in salvation want to have only that which finalizes the death sin brings? James says sin, when it is finished, brings death? The Apostle Paul says worldly sorrow for sin works death. It works in that death we know for sin. After the death of sin takes us, if all we have is worldly sorrow, then such worldliness finalizes that death. It will be so until we can come to the light of having the Godly sorrow needed to bring the blood to cleanse us from all sin. I John 1:7 says the blood only works in the light and O how the body of Christ so needs to understand this.

What is this light in Godly sorrow, this great grief of God? When we sin, God grieves over our separation. In His grief, the Holy Spirit convicts us of God's loss. If we enter the same grief for the sins we fail in, then we have Godly sorrow. Then, in our loss and Godlike sorrow for sin, we turn to the cross. We see the suffering of Jesus. For this sin that has brought the death of separation did He suffer so much pain and sorrow. Our hearts break. Our spirits are crushed and opened to the healing that comes from the bruise of Christ. This is good, but after our healing and restoration comes, we must carry the vision and understanding with us everyday and hour of our lives. Then the full power of God in the cross will work a healing beyond all hope and imagination. This is carrying our cross; even the one Jesus gave us at Golgotha.

Let us understand forever how the sacrifice of Christ had to have His spirit and heart fully broken to bring our healing. Then, like Jesus said, we must carry our cross everyday. Part of carrying our cross is carrying that understanding of what Jesus suffered at the cross' hill everywhere we go. Let us ever see just what pain, suffering, and the bruise it took to bring our healing. Then, as we see and understand the crushing, the breaking of His heart and spirit for us, it would bring a brokenness of heart and spirit to us. This brokenness would not come for sin, but for love in seeing the need we have to be healed and how Jesus suffered to bring it to us. This brokenness from sharing in the sufferings of Christ is needed to be the sacrifices of God.

What am I saying here? I pray the Holy Spirit help me explain it. I pray He will help all to capture just how much Jesus suffered to bring our healing and how seeing it daily should ever make our hearts and spirits of the type of brokenness God would not despise.

As His bruise heals us, the tribulations of life will never break us. This faith will overcome the world. We never will become brokenhearted over trouble.

The greatest place of brokenness of heart and spirit that God will not despise comes from ever seeing the price Jesus paid, the fullness of the bruise that brought His cry of being forsaken. If we sin, we bring Christ's bruise to light in recognizing our sins are what brought this terrible death upon our Lord. However, we can begin to have power over sin, even to fulfilling

Romans 6:14 where sin shall not have dominion over us by the power of the cross. Then our carrying of the cross of Christ, which now is our cross, will bring us ever to see just what it took to heal us. Then, the sorrow of ever seeing the price Christ paid on the cross for us should cause our hearts and spirits ever to be broken before our precious Lord Jesus.

What else could we do but fall down brokenhearted at the need of the sacrifice of God in Christ Jesus on the cross vividly being seen everyday of our lives? What else should happen then that we find the sorrow of heart that breaks our spirits for the most beautiful One that ever lived having to suffer so to heal us?

As I wrote in the introduction, in the tragedies of all time, who can tell of one greater than Jesus needing to suffer so much for our sins, even for our salvation? We weep at the sorrows of life in the great tragedies portrayed in print and screen. How much more sorrow should we have when we see the bruise that came upon Jesus to bring our healing. Our hearts and spirits should ever be broken before Him because of it. The broken heart and spirit that is the sacrifice of God, that God will not despise should only come as we look upon Him whom they pierced. Whether for having sinned or as we walk in our healing, brokenness should arise for seeing the great price that brought our healing. The sacrifices of God are a broken spirit and a broken and contrite heart. They can only come as we see and embrace the suffering and the bruise Jesus took to bring our healing.

Who can look and clearly see without bowing their heads in sorrow for its need. Even more so, if we sin, the grief of God should be our grief. God's grief of sorrow should cover us for not loving Jesus so much as to fulfill the work of the cross in overcoming and being free of sin's dominance. This brokenness over the suffering and bruise of Christ should be carried everyday. Then the oil of healing will come. Then our unity with Jesus will rise. Then the oil will flow from Jesus to His body.

Our unity with Jesus depends upon it. It is as the holy oil was poured out upon the head of the high priest and flowed down from there. The holy oil comes from the crushing of the olive. Therefore, let us let the oil given to us in the crushing of Christ cover our entire being. It will flow by breaking open our hearts and spirits to Him.

CHAPTER SIX

THE NEGATIVE OF THE PICTURE

For some, the negative of Psalm 51:17 will apply? As every picture requires a negative, so the negative of the picture of this verse would read, "An unbroken spirit: an unbroken and non repentant heart, O God, You will despise." God may love you as He loves even the lost, but He will despise an unbroken heart and spirit.

We all know we can love someone even while they do things that we do not love, even despise. In just about any marriage this phenomenon occurs. Beloved, what we do reveals what is in our hearts and spirits. That is why Jesus will judge us by our works. It is so because our works reveal what is in our hearts.

Free your spirit by returning to the cross. Break your heat by looking upon the great price Jesus paid to heal you. Let your heart and spirit break at the sight of our crucified Lord. Then obey Jesus' command to bear the cross wherever you go. Yes, bear Christ crucified in all your days on this earth. If you see the great price Jesus and the Father paid to attain our healing, this surely will break and keep broken your heart and spirit before Him. What wonders our heavenly Father would do for them whose heart and spirit have this brokenness? Some have known of it and some will know. May there be many who have this testimony before the Throne.

The ones who were healed by His bruise know they are to ever have this broken spirit and heart. They ever carry the cross and healing bruise of Christ. God will not despise their sacrifices for Him. This brokenness is to be in us so that God will not despise the sacrifices of our hearts and spirits?

Carry the cross and look upon the whole of what Jesus suffered for you daily. What else can happen but your growth unto loving your God, the Lord Jesus, with all your heart, soul, mind, and strength?

Truly, if you carry your cross, the cross Jesus gave you at the hill, you always will be humbly broken. Yes, you can know the ones who see the price Jesus paid for them. Their sorrow over the need for Jesus to be bruised as He was releases the greatest kind of humility from their broken hearts and spirits. Dare to measure yourself in this matter and seek to see more clearly just how high a price Jesus paid to bring your healing. Yes, measure yourself. See just how much you are healed from the power of the sin that brings death. See how much you are humbled before the great love and sacrifice of our heavenly Father and Jesus Christ.

The work of the bruise must dwell in you. It will keep your spirit broken before God forever. It is the source of all faith for healing and wholeness. If you place your faith in anything else, your faith no longer aligns with the faith of the Father and Jesus Christ. They believed in what the cross would do. Should we believe any less? As you gaze on the greatness of Jesus' sacrifice, as you carry that sacrifice everywhere you go, you will see the flow of healing work mighty miracles in you. Then God's words through Isaiah will attain to its greatest fulfillment. Then His bruise will bring the greatest healing possible. You will be made whole, ever humbled before the love that gave so much to make you that way.

Quote the word. Speak it into the earth and into heaven for it is power. "By His bruise I am healed." Every time you remember the sacrifice of Christ, it can break open your inner man. If you see and embrace the final bruise that Christ took, it will break and keep open your heart and spirit before God. From that humble brokenness, from seeing the bruise and ever humbly receiving it for your healing, you are healed. Truly, soon you will say, "By His stripe, I was healed." Sin no longer will have dominion over you (Romans 6:14). Life will flow. The joy of the kingdom will enter. The unity with Jesus that He travailed for will rise. What words can describe the peace of such a place?

Though these things are a great mystery to some, to you who desire all that is from God, it will become part of your being. God wants you whole. It seems a contradiction, but a broken spirit and a broken and contrite heart before God by ever seeing just how much Jesus suffered to save us will bring that healing and wholeness. Jesus paid the price. You need only receive the fullness of the healing by carrying Jesus Christ and Him crucified everywhere you go.

Then the negative of Psalm 51:17 will not apply. Then God will not despise your heart and spirit even though He loves you.

CHAPTER SEVEN

REVELATION TO REALITY

There is a distance between revelation and reality. The revelation tells us where we are going and even how we should get there. The reality will require us to walk on the road to the destination. Revelation gives us the road map, but only when we travel the road to the destination can we attain to the reality. You have the revelation of Christ's sacrifice. Will you now carry this sacrifice unto being healed in your heart, soul, mind, and body?

You start with the great salvation brought by repentance and calling upon Jesus to save you. This is only the start. Every day afterwards, you must carry the cross, the sacrifice of Christ, unto seeing all your flesh crucified with Him. The more you know of the cross, the more it becomes your cross and the more it can work if you carry it every day. The more you know, the more power resides for you to put all your carnal members that bring you to sin to its death (Colossians 3:5). Then you are daily being healed of the carnal flesh's power to kill and destroy your spiritual life. Then, through daily carrying the cross and remembering the bruise, you ever will remain healed of heart, soul, and mind unto attaining to the prize of the high calling of being part of the first resurrection (Philippians 3).

May our heavenly Father grant us the grace to carry the cross of Christ ever seeing the bruise that brings our healing. To do this in a greater measure, let us now see the thoughts of Jesus in those last three hours upon the cross.

CHAPTER EIGHT

PSALM 143

In Luke 24:44 Jesus said that the Psalms speak of Him and the cross. Let us look into them that reveal the heart and soul of Christ in this day. Let us fellowship with His sufferings as we see Him in His thoughts and feelings on the cross.

Look upon our suffering Lord at this time. He always held a close communion with the Father. He knew what the Father wanted and did it. Jesus walked through every circumstance in victory. Then, in this last day of suffering, something happened. The Father struck a blow that He did not understand. Desolation surrounded Him and entered into His heart.

Psalm 143 touches this moment. In verses 3 and 4 of that Psalm, we see Jesus saying, "For the enemy hath persecuted My soul; he hath smitten My life down to the ground; he hath made Me to dwell in darkness, as those that have been long dead. Therefore is My spirit overwhelmed within Me; My heart within Me is desolate." Jesus spoke these words to His Father while on the cross. Darkness covered His soul even as it covered the land. Therefore, Jesus' Spirit was overwhelmed and His heart had become desolate. The enemy had done his work. Then the crushing silence of the Father came. Can you see the final blow of the Father being so close and doing nothing for three hours? What hope Jesus must have had at His Father's arrival. We see it in that His overwhelmed spirit still took three hours to be broken open. How long would you have lasted?

Psalm 143 shows us Jesus' state at some point after the darkness covered the land. Up to the time the darkness came, Jesus showed confidence as seen in His prayer for them who did not know what they were doing and His response to the thief that sought His salvation. I imagine Jesus prayed these words to His Father as soon as His dwelling place of darkness came before Him. Why should He wait a moment longer after seeing His Father come so close to Him? The thoughts, yes even the prayer must have come just as Jesus' Father's dwelling place centered upon the scene.

Have you not known the same way of it in a trial? While the world looked on, you would have and show a strong face and confident words for you knew you were doing the will of the Lord in a matter. Yet, when you should come close to God in prayer, you let go of that strength to fall upon the mercy and lovingkindness of your Lord and God. Like a child, you would call, even cry out to Him who has the power to deliver and heal you.

Little Johnny falls down in front of his friends. He has some cuts and bruises but he is known for being tough. Therefore, he puts up a good front. He says, "It's no big deal." Still, the neighborhood kids tell him to get some attention. When he arrives home, at the sight of mom, he lets go and tells her how much it really hurts. Jesus too was strong in the face of all that watched Him until His Father arrived. Then, He shared

His sufferings with His heavenly Father. He told Him all that was happening within Him.

There is more in this Psalm. We see our Lord's thoughts as we should continue to read. "I remember the days of old; I meditate on all Your works; I muse on the work of Your hands. I stretch forth My hands unto You: my soul thirsts after You, as a thirsty land. Selah." I see Jesus opening His hands despite the pain to worship His Father in these first moments of His arrival.

Jesus thought upon all the works of His Father. As all His great works came across His mind, it brought the greatest response any man could do. He stretched out the hands of His soul and shared His faith in Him who had come so close.

In some trouble, have you not done the same? You would think upon the things Jesus has done for you. You began to reach out in your soul's desire for comfort and release from your Lord God. This brought you to put forth your hands in praise, desire, and faith in His lovingkindness despite the present struggle. Think about this. How much more would the Son of God do so?

Yes, Jesus thought upon all the Father's works. This had to take some time for Jesus knew so much of what the Father had done. Finally, as the meditation encouraged our Lord, these words reached into the heavens with His outstretched hands. "Hear me speedily, O Lord: my spirit fails: hide not Your face from Me, lest I be like unto them that go down to the pit. Cause me to hear Your lovingkindness in the morning: for in You do I trust: cause Me to know Your way wherein I should walk; for I lift up My soul unto You. Deliver Me, O Lord, from Mine enemies: I flee unto You to hide Me. Teach Me to do Your will; for You are My God: Your Spirit is good: lead Me into the land of uprightness. Quicken Me, O Lord, for Your name's sake: for Your righteousness' sake bring My soul out of trouble."

Would you look and hear this prayer of our precious Savior and would you know that even with this prayer, our heavenly Father still did nothing? What price, what pain, what terrible anguish of soul our Lord must have known to bring us our healing? Can any look upon Him whom they pierced and that our heavenly Father bruised and still prefer sin? Can any see the soul of our Lord in this time and not only be humbled, but desire all the healing of His bruise?

This was the greatest struggle ever faced by any man. It came to its culmination in the last hour upon the cross. It is as Jesus' words in the Psalm reveal. The overwhelmed spirit and desolate heart reached their limits for, though Jesus was the Son of God, He also lived in the finite realm of man.

Look at Jesus on the cross. He was bound and beaten suffering the great weight of the curse and punishment for sin. He saw His Father come upon the scene. Then He began to look up to His Father for deliverance. None came. Within Himself He cried out, "Hear Me speedily, O Father, My Spirit fails." Though Jesus saw His dwelling place, His Father yet was hidden from Him. So, He said, "Hide not Your face from Me . . . Cause Me to hear Your lovingkindness in the morning, for in You do I trust . . . Deliver Me, O Father, from Mine enemies: I flee unto You to hide Me." O, what a prayer of faith! Yet, silence is all that the darkness returned unto Jesus. Even for three hours, the heavens and our heavenly Father was silent to Him.

Jesus waited as the power of sin kept Him bound hand and foot to the cross. He kept His eyes looking up waiting for His Father to move. An hour passed. The pain of the cross and beaten body worked great agony upon His soul and heart. Yet, no word or deed came from His Father. His enemies still surrounded Him. The sins of the whole world continued its destruction. The second hour passed. Still nothing came from those dark clouds except darkness. Sin and death surrounded His heart. They struck His innermost being with the same viciousness as the Jews, the Romans, and the cross attacked Jesus physically. Despair and desolation warred against the heart of our Lord. Now, the third hour was upon Him. His spirit was about to fail. His natural heart was about to cease to beat. Jesus must have thought, "What are you waiting for Father?"

During these three hours, Jesus must have gone through every scripture that He knew that spoke of the cross. He could find none that revealed something that He had missed. Confusion began to enter. Again, the word says Jesus was tempted in all things as we are. Some time in His life, Jesus had to face the test of confusion. The question formed. "Did I miss something? What would make My Father wait so long? Father, why have You forsaken Me? Why have You left Me here when You are so close?" The blow struck deeply into Jesus' heart and now circled His spirit. Confusion led to the test of despair, even the sorrow of heart that would break a spirit.

CHAPTER NINE

PSALM 69

How powerful was this blow of the Father's lack of doing anything being so close? Psalm 69:20 reveals that it broke Jesus' heart. "Reproach has broken My heart; and I am full of heaviness: and I looked for some to take pity, but there was none; and for comforters, but I found none." Add to this how the Father did nothing to comfort or show pity upon His Son and surely such reproach would break any heart.

Brethren, Jesus did look and you and I both know He looked into His Father's dwelling place most of all for that pity and comfort. He found none. No, not even a few raindrops from heaven came to Him to quench His thirst. This scripture clearly tells us of the pain of heart our Lord Jesus had in the moments before His cry of being forsaken.

With us, if we meet tribulation of some sort in doing the will of God, the Holy Spirit somehow confirms, comforts, and encourages us to continue. However, for Jesus, nothing was done even though His Father was so close.

Again, Psalm 69:20 tells us reproach broke the heart of Jesus. How dare I say that this scripture applies directly to Jesus and His heart on the cross? It is because of the following verse attached to it. Verse 21 says, "They gave me also gall for my meat; and in my thirst they gave me vinegar to drink." Of course, this verse of gall and vinegar is a direct reference to the cross. The word, "Also," links this verse about the vinegar with the one before it that says Jesus' heart was broken.

Please carefully note the truth of the matter. Directly attached to the fulfilled verse of the cross about the vinegar is the broken heart of our Lord. Our Lord's heart broke after the Father's dwelling place came upon the scene. The blow of our heavenly Father doing nothing for three hours brought it. Look again upon the reproach our Lord knew in this time. All that man did showed no effect upon His confidence. Then, as the hours passed, the reproach of man added to the seemingly reproaching silence of His Father broke our Lord's precious heart. The truth of it cannot be denied for the holy scriptures show it. Reproach broke Jesus' heart. Can you see the height of suffering Jesus knew to bring His heart to the depth of brokenness?

So many have preached and wondered at the amazing fulfillments of the verse about the vinegar and other prophesies about Jesus' death. It has been proven impossible to put down so many prophecies so many years before even crucifixion was invented and see them all fulfilled except the all powerful God would do it.

Continuing in Psalm 69, we again see the thoughts of Jesus. In verses 14-17 we see our Lord cry out to His Father in secret prayer, "Deliver Me out of the mire, and let me not sink: let Me be delivered from them that hate Me, and out of the deep waters. Let not the waterflood overflow Me, neither let the pit shut her mouth upon Me. Hear Me, O Lord; for Your lovingkindness is good: turn unto Me according to the multitude of Your tender mercies. And hide not Your face from Your servant; for I am in trouble: hear Me speedily."

Again, we see the same thoughts and prayers of seeking a speedy deliverance as in Psalm 143:7. Jesus saw His Father's dwelling place. He looked up and sought deliverance. The blow of silence continued. The Father yet hid in the darkness and Jesus cried out in secret prayer, "Hide not Your face from Your servant for I am in trouble. Hear Me speedily."

Can you see it? Can you imagine it? In all the great times of need, in all the prayers of deliverance of all the saints, in all the hours of darkness surrounding our lives, has anyone known as much travail as these words reveal. O, would you look at the words. "Hide not Your face!" What terror worked for the darkness of the hour? "I am in trouble!" All of the cries of all of the saints in all of time cannot match the heartbreak of this moment. Thus, Jesus again sought His Father saying, "Hear Me speedily!"

What did the Father do? Nothing! Silence was all that He returned to Jesus. Can you imagine the pain? Will you fellowship with Jesus in the matter brokenhearted for the price paid for us? Let us humbly bow down and break our own hearts for the only way to save and heal us forever. Yet, if seeing our Lord in such trouble does not move your heart, cry out for the Almighty God to break it so that He will not despise it.

Do you feel the pain of our Lord Jesus? I pray you are able to fellowship with Him in this being broken before Jesus. If so, Jesus truly will fellowship with you about it.

Again, let us see the anguish of soul, the very pouring out of Christ's soul that Isaiah 53:10 reveals. Isaiah tells of Jesus having done no evil and then he says, "Yet it pleased the Lord to crush Him; He has put Him to grief: when You shall make His soul an offering for sin." Once again, remember John 3:16. It was the Father that gave Jesus. As a father, the greatest thing I have done is in my two sons. Our heavenly Father gave the greatest, most important One in His eternal life to save us because He loved us as He loves Jesus. I pray we can carry this part of the cross. I pray we ever will set before our eyes the sorrow and brokenness Jesus suffered unto it crucifying all our carnal flesh. Then, what can take us away from the love of God flowing in and to us? Though sin once took us away at its slightest beckoning, if we fellowship with Jesus in His suffering, sin will lose its dominion. If, at the least, we ever carry the depth of pain Jesus knew to heal us, truly we will be healed of sin by His bruise.

Before Jesus went to the cross, He knew of the torture man was about to put upon Him. However, He did not know of the blow that was to come to crush Him. If He had, He would not have asked the question why the Father had forsaken Him.

The bruise that brought our healing did not come from man. It pleased the heavenly Father to crush Him when God made His soul an offering for our sins. Jesus' willingness to die and our heavenly Father's need to do nothing brought the bruise that healed us.

Now, the greatest honor we can do Jesus and our heavenly Father is to let His bruise heal us of all sin and death. Let us honor our God by ever seeing and sharing in this greatest time of suffering of any. Let us lift Jesus high in this matter and draw near to Him for it. Yes, and let us never again leave His side for any sin of the world.

We have seen the heart of Christ in Psalm 69. We have seen His thoughts and feelings. Now let us see what I believe to be the very first thoughts upon the mind of our Lord and Savior when the darkness of His Father's dwelling place came upon the scene. The thief has just sought his salvation and Jesus gave it to Him. Immediately afterwards, the darkness formed above Jesus. He watched His Father's dwelling place appear and spoke to Him in prayer saying, "Save Me, O God; for the waters are come in unto My soul. I sink in deep mire, where there is no standing: I am come into deep waters, where the floods overflow Me, I am weary of my crying: My throat is dried: mine eyes fail while I wait for My God." When His Father came so close, Jesus told Him of His sorrow, but there is more.

Jesus continues saying, "They that hate Me without a cause are more than the hairs of Mine head: they that would destroy Me, being mine enemies wrongfully are mighty: then I restored that which I took not away." Truly, for all the good Jesus did, them that called for His crucifixion hated Him without a cause. Yet, as Jesus said, He was restoring that which He did not take away. Adam took away the intimacy we could have had with God. Jesus was restoring it.

Adam took away our soul's union with God. Jesus was restoring it. O, how can we do anything but bow down in sorrow and worship for the price Jesus paid to save us? Still, there is more in this Psalm.

The next verse says, "O God, You know My foolishness; and my sins are not hid from You." With this Psalm so directly connected to the cross, we might wonder how we should understand these words. We do know Jesus took upon Himself all the foolishness and sins of man. He became one with our sins and foolish acts so that we could become one with Him and His Holiness. He became guilty that we could become innocent in Him. We claim our salvation for Jesus taking our sins upon the cross. Jesus would have to have become one with our sins and foolishness to take them away from us. As we call Jesus' righteousness our own, He, to save us, would call our sins His. Then, they would be consumed in the fire of the cross. Thus, our heavenly Father could remove them forever from us who call upon His name. Let us bow down and worship Jesus for His willingness to bear our sins and punishment of being separated from God. Let us worship Jesus for becoming one with our guiltiness, to call it His own so that we can become one with His righteousness and holiness.

We now read of Jesus' awesome prayer after He made Himself one with our sins and foolishness. "Let not them that wait on You, O Lord God of hosts, not be ashamed for My sake: let not those that seek You be confounded for My sake, O God of Israel. Because for Your sake I have borne reproach; shame has covered

My face." On the cross Jesus made this prayer. Can you see Jesus looking out at them who would be confused at His death? His disciples, his mother, the other women at the cross, the multitudes that He healed and helped, all would not understand His death. In the midst of the last three hours of suffering, our Savior prayed for all who knew Him and all who would know Him. Yes, and He prayed even for you.

Will you just stop and think about this prayer of our suffering Savior? For the Father's sake He went to Calvary. Jesus took it all for the Father's sake. Yet, in the midst of the greatest time of trouble of any man, He prays for us. He prays for you.

We might wonder of our times of darkness. Are we as He is here in the world? Do we pray for others in our times of darkness? I pray we all can look upon Jesus' prayer in the darkest hours of our life and be like Him. I know if we are like Him in this, our prayers certainly will be heard.

Let us look again at this prayer. "Let not them that wait on You, O Lord God of hosts, be ashamed for My sake: let not those that seek You be confounded for My sake." Did your faith take great strides towards being perfected in seeing the prayer of Christ for us? Every Christian that truly waits upon God can know that he or she will not be ashamed because of this prayer of Christ on the cross, in the darkest last hours. Every one that seeks God will not be confounded, confused, or counted as lost if they seek God through the crucified and risen One, Jesus Christ.

I Timothy 2:5 says, "There is one God, and one mediator between God and men, the man Christ Jesus." He is the only mediator between God and us. His prayer of mediation on the cross is guaranteed. We will not be ashamed for His sake if we wait upon God. He will not let us become confounded, remain confused, or be counted as lost as we seek Him through the man Jesus Christ. This is a prayer of Christ on the cross. Can any think our heavenly Father would not answer it for us in our waiting upon Him in the dark hours of our lives? Indeed, when we lift up Jesus and the world gives us scorn and mockery, we will not be ashamed. Jesus has prayed it to be so. Wait for the answer and you will see it.

What an awesome prayer Jesus made for us! Yet, it came right in the middle of all His sufferings, even as the bruise of the Father was being laid upon Him. What love! What care! Who cannot humbly bow down seeing Jesus' words for all that would carry the cross in the face of Satan's opposition.

Who could be so faithless as to believe our heavenly Father would fail to eternally honor this prayer? Who could wait upon God and think he or she will bear any shame for it? Who would dare seek God and think he or she would remain confused and confounded by sin's power to bring death when this prayer came in the midst of the greatest suffering any man has ever known? Could you? Only one without any faith in God, His Son, or the work of the cross could deny God would answer his or her seeking for the fullness of the healing that comes through Jesus.

Whether you are young or old, if you believe in Jesus and wait upon God, you will not be ashamed. Whether you are a child or one thought of as elderly, God will not let you be confounded, confused, or lost if you seek God through Jesus Christ and His finished work on the cross. No matter what you have said or done, for Jesus' sake, God will answer the true tears of repentance. Your sins will no longer be a shame upon you. If sin has confounded and confused you, why would you wait a second longer to seek the One who prayed for you on the cross, the One whose every prayer was and will be answered? In all your seeking and waiting, I pray you will know Jesus has already prayed for your answer in the height of His suffering. Who would let sin dominate and confuse them after seeing our suffering Savior make this prayer?

Our heavenly Father is already set to answer Jesus' prayer over our confusion about sin's dominance. All He needs is for you to seek Him and wait upon Him for your healing by His bruise. Our heavenly Father will answer you because of what Jesus said after the He prayed for us who would seek and wait upon Him. He will answer "Because for Your (our heavenly Father's) sake I (Jesus) have borne reproach; shame has covered My face." The shame of the cross, the curse, and the punishment for sin covered Jesus. It was not for Him first that He did this. Rather for the Father's sake, He bore the reproach of our sins. Then He prayed we would not suffer the shame and confusion of having sin dominate and confuse us if we wait upon God.

Who can see this prayer in the midst of Christ's suffering and not be humbled? Who can see Jesus praying with the crown of thorns still cutting into His head and not bow down and worship? Who can see the crucified Lamb looking up to His Father's dwelling place praying for us and not want to unite to Him for all eternity? All glory to the Lamb of God!

Our heavenly Father has had only one purpose in all history. He wants many children in the image of Jesus. We see the whole of this truth in Romans 8:28-29. The only way to have such children is through being born anew through the power of Christ and His sacrifice. The only way to fulfilling the purpose of God in Romans 8:29 is to give our lives to Jesus because He gave His life for us. Then we must grow in the power of the cross unto being conformed unto His death (Philippians 3:10). Then, if we are conformed unto His death, we can enter a full conformation unto His resurrection. We will rise in His image in a body like unto His glorious resurrected one. I know of no healing of body greater than this. Do you?

Every one that Jesus healed when He walked the country of Israel eventually died. Even them that He raised from the dead died. All bodily healings are temporal in this age. Yet, an eternal healing of body will come to them that overcome in fellowshipping with Jesus' sufferings. The first resurrection will bring a healing of body so awesome to them who conform to His death that I marvel at the ones who fail to press to attain to it. When that day of the first resurrection arrives, according to scripture, only the ones that conformed to Christ's death will know the final power of healing by His bruise. It is so because we often will have fellowshipped with His sufferings unto knowing the healing the bruise brings to our heart, soul, mind, and even our temporal body.

I pray you are able to fellowship with Jesus' sufferings revealed in this Psalm. It is full of the understandings of our Lord Jesus' love, thoughts, and pain?

We now have one more thing to learn from it. We must see the verse that again would tell us that the Father is the source of the bruise that has brought our healing.

Further in Psalm 69, Jesus tells of them who knew what they were doing in crucifying the Lord of Glory. Christ gave them His first judgments. Jesus tells of the religious men of Jerusalem that chose to see crucified the Lord rather than eternal life He would have given. We hear the judgments for them who knew what they were doing when they called for Jesus' crucifixion and then He tells us He makes those judgments, "For (because) they persecute Him whom You have smitten." We must take into account the words of our Lord Jesus here. He says the Father has smitten Him. Though the Jews and the Romans have done the work, Jesus looks to His Father's command to go to Calvary as the source of His wounds. Let us look further into this in other Psalms.

CHAPTER TEN

THE GREAT CRY OF CHRIST

Psalm 22 starts with the strongest possible connection to the cross. Verse one reads, "My God, My God, why have you forsaken Me?" In addition, if you would know the follow up thoughts to the cry of Christ, you would read the rest of verse one. There, you would hear Him saying within Himself to the Father, "Why are you so far from helping Me, and from the words of my roaring (groaning)?" Can you hear the second part of the prayer of our Lord coming from within Him? Can you see Him looking into the thick darkness with His appeal for an answer and help?

The cry comes. He shouts of being forsaken. It is a great shout and requires all His strength. Thus, He must pray the rest in silent prayer. In the same desperation of the great shout, He asks God, "Why are you so far from helping Me, and from the words of My groaning." Meditate upon these thoughts of our Lord after His cry. I pray you see the agony and sorrow expressed in Jesus' appeal for an answer.

Read the words again. Look upon Christ praying them after His cry of being forsaken until you see Him saying them to God and thus fellowship with Jesus' sufferings.

CHAPTER ELEVEN

PSALM 22 AND 102

With knowing Psalm 22 speaks of Jesus' suffering on the cross, let us now look at one verse in it. The words that lead up to it are clearly connected to the cross. Then, in verse 15 Jesus says, "My strength is dried up like a potsherd; and my tongue cleaves to My jaws; and You have brought Me into the dust of death." Jesus' cry came at the beginning of the Psalm. His thoughts throughout the first part of the Psalm came after the cry. Before the author returns to give words from God's heart, we see the very thoughts of Christ after His cry.

His strength has dried up like a potsherd. Like a broken piece of pottery no longer able to do anything, so has Jesus said to God and Himself of His vitality and life. His thirst goes beyond description, but He looks up to His Father when He says, "You have brought Me into the dust of death."

Though the instruments were the Romans, Jesus looks at God as the source. In a much smaller way, it is as when dad told you to do something and it all went wrong. Did you blame yourself or did you say, "Dad told me to do it." Your co-worker said to stack the boxes six high. They all fell over. Did you take the blame or did you say to your boss, "He told me to do it." Your boss ordered you to set up the section in a certain manner. His boss comes in and says it is wrong. Do you take the blame or would you say, "He told me to do it this way." When someone else tells us to do something and we do it only to get in trouble for it, we first look to the one who told us what to do to give credit for the wounds we experience emotionally or otherwise.

When a president sends troops into battle, we give credit to him first for the wounded and killed. Though the instrument of their harm comes from the enemy, the president must bear the responsibility for being the one who sent them there. Just so is it with Jesus when He went to the cross.

When our heavenly Father told Jesus His crucifixion was the only way to save us, He set Himself to do the Father's will. Thus, Jesus went by the Father's orders. Jesus would attribute everything that happened afterwards to His command.

We again see this in Psalm 102. As to exactly when these words came, I would think they were Jesus' thoughts and prayers shortly after the darkness that hid His Father appeared. Can you see Jesus looking up into the thick clouds of the sky and saying the words of this Psalm?

"Hear My prayer, O Lord, and let My cry come unto You. Hide not Your face from Me in the day when I am in trouble; incline your ear unto Me: in the day when I call answer Me speedily. For My days are consumed like smoke, and My bones are burned as in a hearth, My heart is smitten, and withered like grass; so that I forget to eat My bread. By reason of the voice of My groaning my bones cleave to My skin. I am like a pelican in the wilderness: I am like an owl of the desert. I watch, and am as a sparrow alone upon the housetop. Mine enemies reproach Me all the day; and they that are mad against Me are sworn against Me. I have eaten ashes like bread, and mingled My drink with weeping. Because of Your indignation and your wrath: for You have lifted Me up, and cast Me down."

Psalm 102:1-10

After Jesus expressed the great pain and sorrow He felt upon the cross, He said the Father lifted Him up and cast Him down. Jesus gave His life to our heavenly Father's will. Though the religious leaders bear their guilt for they desired to see Jesus crucified and chose to be part of His crucifixion, He went forward to save us by the Father's bidding. Thus Jesus said, "You have lifted Me up, and cast Me down."

The Psalm continues with praise and worship leading Jesus to think of just what our heavenly Father was doing at that moment. In verses 19-20 Jesus says, seemingly to encourage Himself, "He has looked down from the height of His sanctuary; from heaven did the Lord behold the earth; to hear the groaning of the prisoner."

Imagine the moment the thick clouds of darkness centered around Jesus on the cross. He looks up and expresses His feelings as seen in this Psalm 102. Then He believes and says to Himself His Father will hear Him as He beholds Him.

What hope must have risen in our Lord in the first moments of darkness? Look at Him breathing in the cooled air due to His Father's presence above Him. His love and desire to be united to Him must have been greatly encouraged. Thus, the prayers telling of His great pain and loneliness, even as a sparrow on the rooftop, did ascend through the clouds into the presence of His Father. How could any father hear such prayers and do nothing? For His love of you and me, our heavenly Father did it. May we ever embrace our Lord Jesus and our heavenly Father with such appreciation, gratitude, and love for He first loved us and proved it in the cross.

"He has looked down from the height of His sanctuary; from heaven did the Lord behold the earth; to hear the groaning of the prisoner." Yet, instead of deliverance and reunion, our heavenly Father says and does nothing and He did that for three hours. Surely, the great hope of Christ not only was crushed, but all His inner man now also felt the same crushing that the cross was doing to His body. Can you see the great suffering blow the Father gave Jesus by arriving on the scene as He did and then saying and doing nothing?

Jesus received each stripe, blow, and atrocity of punishment as fulfilling the Father's will. The Jews beat and mocked Him. Jesus' thoughts centered on the knowledge that He was doing the Father's will. Pilate ordered the scourging. Blow after blow fell upon our Lord's back. Jesus took each one of them saying to Himself it was the Father's will for Him. The cry of the Jewish people came saying they had no king but Caesar and His blood will be upon them and their children. Thus, the order came to crucify Him. The

Roman battalion came together to torture Jesus. They beat him, spit on him, pulled out His beard, and put the crown of thorns upon Him. Then they took a thick cane and hit Him on the head repeatedly until He was unrecognizable. Finally, they crucified Him. Yet, after they lifted Him up, Jesus' thoughts were strong to think, "You have lifted Me up, and cast Me down." Jesus knew He was in the Father's will. Thus, with confidence, love, grace, and such mercy, He asked for the forgiveness of them who knew not what they were doing.

Three hours of the torture of the cross and ridicule of all around Him passed. Then, the thief asks for salvation and receives it with such grace and confidence from our Lord Jesus. He still knows He is in the Father's will. At each blow of the road to the cross, we can hear Jesus thinking, "I am doing Your will Father. I am following the will of My Father. He has sent Me here and I must finish the course of it." Then the Father came upon the scene. His dwelling place changed the air around our Lord. He knew His Father was so close and hoped in His deliverance. "Hear me speedily!" was His spirit's cry.

Yet, the Father struck the bruise of doing nothing. This went on until Jesus knew His physical life was about to end. As He felt His physical life almost over, He desperately needed to be reunited with His Father who was so close and yet still separated from Him. Thus, His spirit broke and He made the cry all heard and the silent prayer that followed as to know why He was about to die without that reunion. What had He missed? Can you yet still hear that cry and silent appeal?

"My God, My God, why have You forsaken Me? Why are you so far from helping Me, and from the words of my groaning?"

Psalm 22:1

Truly, "It pleased the Lord to bruise Him. He has put Him to grief." All that man did to Jesus certainly crushed His body, but none of it made Jesus wonder as to what our heavenly Father was waiting for in delivering Him from His suffering. He knew He was in the Father's will and all that had happened was because of Him. Though His body was brutally beaten and destroyed, Jesus remained strong in His Father's purpose to see Him crucified until the blow of three hours of darkness and silence had passed.

All that confidence withered away as the crushing blow of the Father's silence struck. That bruise brought our healing. By His bruise, by the wound, by the stripe of our heavenly Father doing nothing for three hours, we are healed. Glory to Jesus!

Set this bruise before you at every prayer and need of healing for your spirit, heart, soul, mind, and body. Seeing the price Jesus paid to bring our healing will give you confidence that it is Jesus' will that you are healed. It will come first in spirit and heart at new birth. Then His bruise will work out that healing in our souls. Finally, to them who are healed, spirit, heart, and soul, healing becomes available to the body in a greater way, even unto the greatest healing of the first resurrection. How can we think Jesus wants us anything but whole with such a great price that He paid in receiving the final bruise? Where is your faith in this matter?

CHAPTER TWELVE

JESUS' SPIRIT BROKEN

Psalm 69:20 shows us Jesus' heart was broken on the cross. The pain of the last three hours must have been powerful. The word says it broke our Lord's heart. The blow came from the Father. He drew close and did nothing until Jesus cried wanting to know if He missed something.

By the third hour of darkness, the ordeal of the cross truly brought desolation and breaking to Jesus' heart. Isaiah 53:5 says that Jesus was crushed for our iniquities. Yes, by the third hour the blow of our heavenly Father crushed His heart.

The Bible prophetically recorded the complete desolation brought upon Jesus' heart and it gives us detail about the bruising of His spirit too. The last area of the Son of God to be attacked was Jesus' spirit. Did Jesus despair of life or did the faith of the Son of God rise up to seek God?

Jesus knew death for every man. Death from the corruption of sin entered every part of Him. His heart felt the desolation of death. Desolation's despair must have covered His entire being. The desolation now turned to the only part of Him that was not broken. It turned to His Spirit. Look into the moments before that loud cry came. Look closely at your suffering Savior.

They destroyed Jesus' body. They beat it beyond recognition. They nailed it to the cross. The cross took all His ability to use His body. It held Him captive. Just so does sin do to all in its grip. Yet, for all that, Jesus confidently went forward. Then the Father drew close hidden behind that thick darkness. He struck the blow of doing nothing. The realm of separation and hopelessness that sin causes entered into His soul and mind. The question must have arisen, "What is He waiting for? Why is He not doing anything?"

Jesus faced temptation in all things. The question must have been there for Jesus needed to be tempted with confusion. "What are you waiting for Father?" Confusion soon moved into the depths of despair and the temptation to accuse God it causes some to do. The first hour passed. Then a second hour worked upon Jesus' inner being. As the end of the third hour neared, Jesus' heart began to enter the fullness of desolation. His natural heart was failing even as His spiritual heart was broken.

All the signs said God had forsaken Him. It brought desolation to His entire being except His spirit. However, at this point of crushing, the sin and its' power to bind and kill began to attack Jesus' spirit. Yet, the Father still waited.

The result of sin is complete captivity. We see its expression in the binding of Jesus' hands and feet by the nails. The pain and bondage that sin produces has the very effect we see Jesus went through. Jesus suffered our death for we know Jesus said them who have not His salvation will be bound hand and foot and thrown into the pain of outer darkness where God is not. Jesus' death on the cross reveals the death all who have not His salvation will know. I pray this gives you more power to witness to the lost.

When we sin, we also know a death of separation. This pain begins to cover our entire being unless the conscience has become seared. The agony of separation from God becomes reality if we fall short in some sin. Just so, in some small measure, we can know the great pain of our Lord's separation upon the cross.

Just as sin destroys us, so did all the sins of the whole world destroy Jesus' body, His soul, and His heart? Sin completely binds us in our ability to fellowship with God and each other. Just so did sin bring the blow of the silence of the Father in those last three hours. In the natural, Jesus was bound hand and foot on the cross. Spiritually, the cross bound His heart and soul. Though He could see His Father's dwelling place right next to Him, the cross and the bearing of our sins bound Him and kept Him from His Father.

Just as Jesus knew how close His Father was, so also do we know that God dwells in us ever so close. Yet, when we sin, we know the same separation and darkness between our Lord and us. Sin brings in a complete binding as it bound Jesus on the cross.

Through the pain of our failures, we can feel a small taste of the greatness of suffering that Jesus knew. Yes friend, Jesus has felt the pain of separation that we feel when we sin. Only it was billions of times more intense for He felt it for so many.

Jesus looked into the thick darkness. He almost could see His Father behind the clouds. Yet, the separation continued for God was striking the blow of doing nothing. What pain, what agony to see His Father do nothing as all within Him was being crushed.

What happened at the end of the three hours? Jesus' spirit had met the result of sin. Every part of His outer and inner man except His spirit had been beaten, crushed, and bound ever so painfully. Jesus' spirit now met the full force of that moment.

You see dear reader; Jesus knew His body was about to die. He felt the death coming and He was still separated from His Father. In the plan of the ages, He was not supposed to go down into the pit separated from His Father.

Psalm 28:1 records the thoughts of Christ at the moment before His awesome cry of being forsaken. Jesus felt a fear He did not expect. In Psalm 28:1 we see Jesus saying, "Unto You will I cry, O Lord My rock; be not silent to Me: lest, if Thou be silent to Me, I become like them that go down into the pit." Jesus knew He was about to die without reuniting with His Father. We see Him expressing it ever so clearly in the Psalms. Think about these thoughts in the written word and let us be in awe at the death that has brought us our salvation and healing.

The terrible pressure of waiting for three hours after seeing His Father's dwelling place and being bound to the cross had done its work. Jesus' Spirit broke. Up to this point, He waited in silence. However, when His Spirit broke, what was inside came pouring out like a rushing river. It flooded His heart, poured into His soul, covered His mind, and drove out that awesome loud cry and silent appeal. Jesus was seeking His God. If He had lost His Sonship for missing something, God was still His God and He sought Him with all His being.

Up to this day and these last three hours, nothing had the power to break Jesus' spirit. Many things flowed out from it. However, nothing ever came that was the result of being broken apart. It is as the vial of sweet perfume that needed one powerful blow to break it open to let all know of its contents. Jesus' Spirit was broken and out poured all that was within Him. Jesus' Spirit met the full force of the viciousness of man, sin, and death, but it was not enough. It took the blow of the Father drawing so close and doing nothing to break open His precious spirit. It was at the cry. We know it was the moment of Jesus' spirit breaking. It was so for we see the purest of faith pouring out of Him.

How terrifying a moment this was? What happened after those three hours of watching His Father's dwelling place return nothing but silence? Jesus' spirit broke. Can you stop and dwell on the struggle of knowing the silence of His Father, the viciousness of sin, the curse, and the fullness of all these to break our Lord's spirit? Truly, He did take upon Himself sin and its curse. A wonder, even great awe, should well up in our hearts as we touch this moment that Jesus faced for us.

Many do not understand this cry of Christ. They do not know whether the desolation won or not? By faith they trust it did not, but still they wonder as to whether our Lord stumbled in this moment or not. No, Jesus did not fail. What Jesus spoke to the Father came from the flow of what dwelled in His spirit. Again, Hebrews 11:6 says that faith believes that God is and that He is a rewarder of them that seek Him. Jesus fully believed in God's reality and sought Him for the help and reward of an answer as to why He was about to die without them being reunited.

Jesus sought His God for an answer? If our Lord had cried out in any form of rejection toward God, He would have failed and sin would have won. If words of anger, frustration, accusation, or words of self-defense had come, He would have failed true faith. Jesus' spirit broke and yet still overcame for He did not sin in word. He overcame sin and death in that cry of faith. He believed and sought God.

Can anyone do anything but wonder in great wonder over this? There does not exist a word to describe the awe we should feel in just what Jesus suffered to overcome sin and death for us. I see it but cannot fully express the wonder of it yet still, can you?

Listen to that loud voice reaching through all eternity. Hear the silent appeal that only the Father heard at that moment. Hear the voice of faith reaching heavenward to His God only a few feet away. Listen to the words echo across all the earth to every soul that would turn an ear to hear. "My God, My God, why hast Thou forsaken Me? Why are You so far from helping Me, and from the words of My groaning?"

Yes, the curse of the cross is the result of sin. It tried to choke out all the hope of our Lord. Yes, He felt despair's darkening desolation break His heart. Yes, the blow of the Father doing nothing attacked and broke open His spirit. From that moment of breaking, what dwelled within His spirit poured out into His entire being and drove Him to shout and make His silent appeal. He spoke nothing evil. He gave only words of faith. Praise our Savior and Lord!

Yes, Glory to our Lord Jesus! He overcame for He cried out in faith believing God is and that He is a rewarder of them that seek Him. Sin lost all in this moment. Let us bow the knees of our hearts and give Him all praise, honor, love, and dedication.

Truly, the pain was awesome; yet, the Lord overcame the darkest moment in all history.

It would take the most awful of trials to bring Jesus to a place that He would think He might have missed something. It would take a terrible blow to make Him wonder if the Father had left Him to die upon the cross not yet reunited to Him. He absolutely must have had to face this blow to make His sacrifice for us complete. Why did the Father leave Jesus on that cross while He set only a few feet away behind that darkness? The sacrifice would not have been complete if Jesus' spirit did not break to show all what perfect faith dwelled inside of Him and open the way for God to pour out that faith into us. Isaiah truly said it. "By His bruise we are healed." If we believe in the bruise, the fountain of Christ's faith begins to flow into us. O, do you see it? We are to have the faith of the Son of God through the work of the cross.

When God laid upon Jesus all the sins of the world, He did it that Jesus would taste the death of those sins for every man. The result of sin is death. The result of death is separation from God. Again, Jesus' death on the cross reveals what hell and the Burning Lake of Fire will be like. Even so, Jesus entered it for us and overcame so we would not need to know it eternally.

God brought Jesus to feel, know, and become one with the fruit of sin. Think of it! Death pressed into Jesus. God allowed Him to face it. He met the fullness of the result of sin. It brings complete destruction to all within us. It is complete separation from God. Yes, sin brings the fullness of death.

It had to be for you and me to have a perfect advocate in Christ. He had to face more than the weight of sin. The sin had to attack Him with all the viciousness it had. Truly, it did. The sacrifice of the cross, at the cry of Christ, was complete. Jesus not only took upon Himself all sin, but He faced its power to bring complete despair, desolation, and death to a heart. Then He overcame it in its final thrust on His spirit. Let us give all the glory, honor, praise, and worship to Jesus for His sacrifice on the cross.

Upon that moment of breaking all creation hung. Our salvation waited for it. God waited for it. And Jesus was perfected by it. The writer of Hebrews tells us that, "We see Jesus, who was made a little lower than the angels for the suffering of death, crowned with glory and honor; that He by the grace of

God should taste death for every man. For it became Him, for whom are all things, in bringing many sons unto glory, to make the captain of their salvation perfect through sufferings." What does this scripture mean? Jesus was born perfect. He lived a perfect life. He was without sin. He always did what pleased the Father. Where can any lay an accusation of Him ever sinning? Yet, according to this scripture, He was not yet perfect. He needed to pass through the fire of the sacrifice perfectly to be made perfect. That could only come through a breaking of His spirit according to Psalm 51:17.

Truly, Jesus' greatest suffering came in those last three hours on the cross. Through this bruise of the Father doing nothing, He was perfected. Through this bruise caused by the blow of His Father coming so close and doing nothing, we are healed.

Again, it is even as Isaiah 53:10 says, "Yet, it pleased the Lord to bruise Him; He has put Him to grief: when You shall make His soul an offering for sin." It pleased our heavenly Father to put that one bruise upon Christ Jesus to bring about our healing. It was for us that Jesus died and for us the Father struck the blow that would break His spirit.

That breaking came from one crushing blow. The one blow of Jesus' Father being so close and doing nothing broke open all that was in Jesus' spirit. Through the stripe of the Father doing nothing for those three hours, our sacrifice was perfected and our healing came. By His stripe, we were healed. Yes, His bruise makes us whole. All glory to the Lamb of God and the Father who sent Him for us.

In that breaking moment, all that was in His Spirit rushed out into His being. As a dam would break and flood the land around it, so what was in Jesus' spirit flooded His entire being. All that dwelled in His Spirit was faith. There was no evil in there. Therefore, all that could come forth were words of faith. His Spirit broke and Jesus spoke. He believed in His God and sought Him.

Psalm 51:17 confirms this truth. It shows by the written word of God the fact that in order to perfect Jesus through perfecting this sacrifice on the cross, His spirit needed breaking. What can we do but break our own hearts over the need for such to happen to Jesus, the Bright and Morning Star, to save us?

Let us now look to see exactly what happened after Jesus cried out in a loud voice and made the silent prayer asking why?

CHAPTER THIRTEEN

THE PSALM OF PSALMS

For three hours, Jesus watched the dark clouds above Him. He knew that the thick clouds hid His Father.

After three hours of that darkness, Jesus broke forth with His most awesome cry. He shouted with a loud voice. What terror surrounded Him at that moment, we can only imagine from the descriptions we have seen from the written word. This we know. The power of the Father doing nothing to deliver Jesus for those three hours tore into Him as a lion would tear apart a lamb.

We have seen some of the thoughts that raced through Jesus' mind in the moments before His cry, but the word of God gives us even more of them? Listen to Jesus' thoughts given by the Holy Spirit and recorded in Psalm Eighteen.

There we see Jesus on the cross thinking, "The cords of death are surrounding Me." Death tied Jesus secure. He knew His body was near death. We can see Jesus questioning why His Father yet waited. He thought, "The torrents of ungodliness terrified Me." Satan, all his hordes, and the men that crucified Him, all taunted Him. They crucified Jesus and brought Him near death. Add this to taking upon Himself the ungodliness of all the sins of the world, and I think Jesus being terrified would describe it about right.

Psalm 18 then shows Jesus thinking, "The cords of Sheol are surrounding Me. The snares of death are confronting Me." To think such thoughts, Jesus must have felt the ropes of death tightening around His physical heart. He saw Himself beginning the journey into death and hell without His union with His Father and His Holy Spirit. Thus, He could know that He fulfilled the sacrifice.

Think of Jesus' feelings! He was about to die still separated from His Father. He felt all the power of death about to take Him. This terror brought the question of why His Father was leaving Him to die without knowing that He fulfilled the needs of the sacrifice. How can He rise again unless the Spirit that will raise Him is united to Him? He became so pressed in His position that when He shouted His cry, He called out to His God rather than His Father. Again, if He had failed as Adam and lost His Sonship, He knew that the Father was still His God. Thus, the question "Why" came in His loud cry. If He had missed something, perhaps He yet could correct it. This contrition flowed in His question and thus His broken heart also was perfectly contrite.

To reveal how great the terrors Jesus faced were, we must rely on the Word. His terror was enough to create the thoughts of Psalm 18. These thoughts climaxed in His loud cry. Psalm Eighteen verse six records the moment. In it Jesus said, "In My distress I called upon the Lord, and cried to My God for help." Jesus' thoughts that He might die still separated from His Father must have given Him the most terrible of terrors. So great did the terror of that moment reach into Christ that in His distress He made His cry seeking why God was so far from Him.

Jesus was perfect, even perfectly man. As a man, He faced all the temptations we know only in the most terrible of ways on the cross. Just as you feel, struggle, are pained, and in distress, so was He. Not only should we see how greatly He suffered and share in them, but also what great confidence we should have knowing He has felt, experienced, and overcome all that we face in a smaller measure. Does this not just lower your eyes in thought over the many times we were distressed and fell short of having a perfect faith in God? Let us now ever lift our eyes towards heaven and wait upon Him. We will not be ashamed for it.

Returning to the moment of Jesus' appeal for an answer, we see He knew God heard His cry. We know for He said, "He heard My voice out of His temple, and My cry for help came before Him, even into His ears." How did He know God heard His cry? He must have been able to see in the Spirit. To say that His Father heard Him meant He saw His Father stir the darkness.

Jesus could see Satan and all his demons. Again, Psalm Twenty-two reveals the cross. In that Psalm, we hear Jesus saying, "Many bulls of Bashan have encircled Me. They open wide their mouth at Me, as a ravening and a roaring lion." For Jesus to know such of them, He must have been able to see them.

For a few hours, Satan thought he had won and taunted the son of man. However, terror began to form in our Lord's thoughts when He felt death begin to surround Him. Finally, Jesus cried to His God for help. O, do you see this awesome moment in its truth and reality? Jesus did not accuse God, but rather sought His help.

As to what happened in the natural and in the spirit, Jesus could only watch for the cross still held Him in its grip. However, by the things written in that Eighteenth Psalm, a psalm of David, we can see what Jesus saw. Jesus cried out and said of the cry that God "heard My voice out of His temple, and My cry for help came into His ears. Then the earth shook and quaked; and the foundations of the mountains were trembling and were shaken, because He was angry." The people around the cross felt the earthquake, but saw nothing else. Everything else that happened, revealed in this most expressive psalm, happened in the spirit. Jesus watched it happen and from it knew that His sacrifice was finished.

In a loud voice, Jesus cried and soon afterward saw the wrath of God. The earth shook and "Smoke went up out of His nostrils, and fire from His mouth devoured; coals were kindled by it." Now that is wrath! Picture a man so angry that smoke comes out of his nose. See him so full of wrath that he opens his mouth and fire pours out of it. God was angry. For the first time, the fullness of God's wrath was seen. The fire that came out of God's mouth burned against Satan and his demons. It ignited their coal black hearts. It ignited great terror in them. Never before has God revealed such anger. Never in all recorded history will we find such wrath.

Psalm Eighteen continues showing what God did with that anger. It says, "He bowed the heavens also, and came down with thick darkness under His feet. And He rode upon a cherub and flew; and He sped upon the wings of the wind. He made darkness His hiding place, His canopy around Him. Darkness of waters, thick clouds of the skies. From the brightness before Him passed His thick clouds, hailstones and coals of fire." Now that is a big change from the past three hours. For three hours, God quietly waited. He waited so close that all could see the darkness that hid Him. However, the moment the sacrifice was complete, God flew on the wings of the wind. From the moment Jesus cried revealing His spirit was broken, the Father immediately moved. It looks to me that the Father was in a big hurry.

It seems God hid all, except the earthquake, from those around Jesus. However, Jesus saw it and knew His Father was answering His cry. Until this moment, even Satan had no idea that all the brightness of our heavenly Father dwelled behind those thick clouds of the sky. Suddenly, he saw God move and it terrified him. Ah, can you see Satan and his devils turn in sudden terror? Picture it and know the devil hates anyone to see it, but there is more.

At that moment, "The Lord also thundered in the heavens, and the Most High uttered His voice, hailstones and coals of fire." What did God say? By the Spirit and the word of God, the Father thundered, "It is finished!" Within that term, we know God is saying the price has been paid and all is complete. However, our heavenly Father was not making a doctrine here. He was quickly proclaiming an end to the ordeal of our Lord Jesus Christ. Let us rejoice in knowing Jesus heard the thundering voice of His Father telling Him and Satan, "It is finished."

What greater words could God say to Jesus than "It is finished?" Picture the wrath, look upon the rushing wind of the Father's Spirit hurrying to the scene, and listen to the voice of God forever proclaiming, "It is finished!" God's voice thundered as He came. He spoke in flight as a bear growling before He attacks.

How can we not weep and rejoice for seeing our Lord at this moment? Our emotions are moved for we see the release Jesus must have known. We rejoice for we see the moment He heard of His victory. The Father thundered out the words, "It is finished!" Jesus heard His answer. He knew the sacrifice was complete. O what releasing peace He must have felt! What joy came into His whole being through hearing those precious words from His Father? The Father said, "It is finished!" and Jesus took a great rest into His heart and soul. Can you see this awesome moment of our salvation?

Later Jesus repeated these words for all to hear. You might ask, "How can you dare say with confidence that Jesus heard and later repeated the words, "It is finished." I say it from the principle that Jesus said that He hears from His Father and then He speaks. He did not say anything on His own. For Jesus to say, "It is finished," He first had to hear it from His Father. Think of it.

God thundered, "It is finished." His love touched Christ and His wrath aimed at Satan and his devils at the same moment. Psalm 18 says that, "He sent out His arrows, and scattered them, and lightning flashes in abundance, and routed them." The gospels tell us nothing of these things. They definitely occurred in the spirit. The angels, Satan, the demons, and Jesus saw them, but, according to the account in the gospels, the people near the darkness and dark clouds seemingly saw none of it. O glory to God, now you can see this moment when God scattered Satan and his hordes. God's mighty lightning bolts routed them. God's arrows were lightening flashes in abundance in the spirit. Imagine it and let even the tears of rejoicing come for, "It is finished."

Jesus saw them that tormented Him now terrified. Perhaps this is the first time ever that any saw the whole of the wrath of God. Glory to His name!

CHAPTER FOURTEEN

THE FOUNDATIONS OF THE WORLD

Before the devil and his demons could escape into their holes or hell itself, Psalm 18 says, "The channels of water appeared, and the foundations of the world were laid bare at Thy rebuke, O Lord, at the blast of the breath of Thy nostrils." Yes, they saw the foundations of the world. Satan and his demons saw for the first time the Lamb slain from the foundation of the world.

God set foundations upon which the world was to build. Through the many sacrifices of Old Testament, God established the foundations to lead to Christ's sacrifice. Noah built upon the foundation as seen in the sacrifice that he offered after he left the ark. Abraham built upon that sacrifice as we view his offerings in Old Testament. To Israel, Moses brought the foundation sacrifices and its tabernacle. They were all types of Christ and Him crucified. Together, as many foundations, they revealed the Lamb to come that would take away the sins of the world. Finally, Jesus came to fulfill all the foundational sacrifices. As Satan and all with him fled the great anger of God, they saw the foundations. They saw all the fulfillments of all the sacrifices in Jesus' work on the cross. God laid it bare before all the angels and demons. They saw the crucified Jesus Christ as fulfilling all the sacrifices that held up the world. By it, God allowed all to exist. We can but wonder as to what agony this sight caused

Satan. Is there a smile coming to your face in this? There is one on me as I write.

The Apostle Paul said, "For no man can lay a foundation other than the one which is laid, which is Jesus Christ." Yes, that which God hid in the sacrifices He now showed. He revealed them all fulfilled in Jesus to Satan and His demons. They saw how all the sacrifices were fulfilled in Christ Jesus our Lord. They saw Jesus Christ. They saw the sacrifice upon which all men who desire the only salvation of God would build. At this moment, God laid the foundations established by all the sacrifices of Old Testament bare before Satan and his devils. At that moment, Satan knew He was defeated. Can we shout victory with a wonder filled heart over seeing Satan fleeing the wrath of God and seeing his defeat? Satan, who is so subtle in evil, had no clue in his sinister joy of being able to torture Jesus. Then the channels of the water of the cross' work were seen. Then the foundations of all those sacrifices were shown. Can we find words to describe Satan's grief? What a sight it must have been?

CHAPTER FIFTEEN

WHAT EFFECT THIS CROSS OF CHRIST

Now, let us ask what are we doing with the cross? Though we would rejoice in the scene of Satan fleeing in defeat, he still presses to make the cross of no effect today.

Some have wanted a crossless gospel. They build on Jesus Christ's sayings. They teach principles and ways to get what they want, but they are building on the wrong foundation. Jesus Christ is the sacrificed Lamb. Jesus Christ and the sacrifice are one. You cannot have Jesus without embracing the sacrifice of the cross. Jesus Christ is the sacrifice. Thus, if you build without the crucified Christ, you build on the wrong foundation.

Multitudes of others have built upon the true foundation, but fail to build with the foundation. What we build on the foundation must have the same material as the foundation. As the city and the singular street of Jerusalem are made of pure gold, so must be the foundation. If we build with the spiritual gold of Christ and Him crucified, we build with the golden way of the cross. Why else would Jesus tell us to carry our cross everyday? Our cross can only be the one Jesus gave us at Calvary. No other cross will ever bring us to be crucified with Jesus. If the cross should not be part of our building, why did Paul preach about dying daily? He told the Philippians he did everything to be conformed to Christ's death so that he might attain to the first resurrection of the dead. Think about it! We must build on the foundation with the same golden material of Christ and the cross that is the foundation.

If our building upon the foundation of Christ fails to have the work of the cross in all of it, then we will be building with the wood, hay, and stubble that God will consume in the fires of the Great White Throne Judgment. Let us understand that a crossless gospel, one without the blood and crucifixion in all that we do, is one without Jesus Christ, the foundation of God. The Apostle Paul proved this to the Galatians for the sacrifice, the Lamb, and the King of kings are one. He is the foundation and, to build properly on Him, you must build with Him and His work on the cross.

Let us embrace the sacrifice everyday. Let us know Jesus Christ and Him crucified. Let us carry all of Him everywhere we go. Let us know Him as the mighty Lord of all and the Lamb. Let us build upon the foundation that God laid bare in that moment. Let us build upon the crucified Christ and with the crucified Christ.

What we do are as the pearls and precious jewels of God in progress. A jewel must have some type of setting to be made of any great value and use. The gold and silver of Christ's nature and work of the cross must be where we seek God to set all that we do. If we build by setting ourselves and our deeds deeper and deeper into the work of the cross of Christ, the jewels set into the gold and silver of Christ will shine bright in any test of fire.

If we put our faith and trust in building anything excluding the finished work of Christ on the cross, we are building with the wood, hay, and stubble of man. Paul wrote of these and the final test of fire in I Corinthians Three. All must start at new birth by repenting and believing in Christ and His sacrifice for us. Then, for not building with the cross, multitudes build with wood, hay, and stubble.

Some men are as solid as wood in their lives and preaching. They accept Christ and His sacrifice for their salvation, but then they outwardly do all their Christian laws in their strength. Thus, consciously or unconsciously, they trust their works for their place in Christ. They are so solid that you can lean upon them and know that they will hold you up. Knock on their wood and they sound solid. The winds of the world or Satan have little power over them. Still, the object of their faith is what they have done and are in themselves. When they stand before the Lord and the test of fire comes, all will turn to ashes and be blown away forever.

Others are like hay. When you compact them together, as in a bale, they have substance and strength. Yet, they need the wire of church oversight to stay solid and strong. If you should remove an individual piece of hay from the bale, the wind would blow it around wherever it wishes. Just so do many stand solid and strong amongst the brethren, but when alone they are taken by whatever wind of doctrine or sin that tempts them. What they are and have done will burn quickly in any test of fire.

Lastly, we meet the stubble. The churches of the stubble saints have no substance. They have nothing solid and become blown about by whatever doctrine or direction their carnal desires take them. These will have nothing connected to the foundation. When gathered together for the bonfire of the last day, all that they are and did will disappear very quickly. Let us pray for them that they still will be saved by the fire according to I Corinthians 3:15.

Let us examine ourselves and see what we are building upon the foundation of Christ and Him crucified. Let us deeply examine ourselves and see if we are building upon Christ and the cross. Again, Paul warned all in I Corinthians Three of the test of fire. I tell you the truth. Only those who set their doings into the gold and silver of Christ and His work on the cross will find anything to remain. If we put our trust in what we can do and what we have done, we will see our works consumed. If the object of our faith is in anything else other than Christ and the cross, we will fall prey to the fire.

However, if all we do sets its dependence and faith upon Christ, Him crucified, and His grace, we will be like fine jewelry set in the purest of gold and silver. We might yet fulfill the scriptures and be conformed unto Christ's death. Let us forever know the Apostle Paul told the Philippians and now us that conformation to Christ's death must happen for us to have any hope to attain to the first resurrection of the dead. This is God's word and I pray for mercy upon all that change it.

May the grace of Christ, given to us at the cross, flow even more. May grace remove us from the wooden way of putting our faith in what we do to what Jesus has done. May His grace keep us from being blown about by every wind of doctrine set for the fires. Yes, we ask Jesus to multiply His grace to teach us to make all our faith to rest only on the foundation of the finished work of our Lord Jesus.

Let us now return to the scene where God's rebuke revealed the foundation of the world to Satan and his demons.

In that one moment, God opened to the devil and his demons the foundation. It came "At Thy rebuke, O Lord, at the blast of the breath of Thy nostrils." God blew away the coverings that hid His foundation. What an awesome moment that was.

Now, Satan may try to cover that foundation in his scheming ways and man may try to build a woody religion on it. However, the foundation of the sacrifice of the Lamb remains open to all that desire it.

Jesus watched God come in great wrath. Jesus heard God's voice thunder the words that the sacrifice was complete, that, "It is finished." What joy, what peace, what rest they must have given our Lord.

Do you see the greatness of that moment? From the written word, we know He heard the words and saw the lightning and witnessed the arrows scatter every demon. Satan fled as a whimpering dog with his tail between his legs. Does not the sight of it bring joy to your heart? Still, I now will tell you the greatest wonder and joy filled scene of all history.

Psalm 18:16 then tells us that God, "Sent from on high, He took Me; He drew me out of many waters." How we should rejoice over this scene. As a father tenderly brings a hurt child into his arms, so our heavenly Father brought Jesus into His spiritual arms. That is, the Father and the Son were One again.

Finally, verse 19 lets us know the greatness of the reunion of Jesus and the Father. "He brought Me forth also into a large place; He delivered Me, because He delighted in Me." What more can any say of this awesome moment in history? For three hours, the Father hid behind the darkness. Now He no longer needed to hide. He sent from on high. He took Jesus. He drew Him out of the waters of death by becoming One with Him again. What larger place do you know than again being united with the One who inhabits the whole universe and beyond? What peace, what joy, what wonder must have flowed into our Lord's spirit and soul. The word of God tells us of the great victory Jesus knew after He shouted His cry for help. The gospels reveal a peace around Jesus after His great shout. This could only come if He knew the sacrifice was finished. At some point after the cry, Jesus and our heavenly Father were reunited and one again. All the power and glory of the Father again dwelled in our precious Lord Jesus. Thus, He could go to preach to the spirits below in paradise once again fully one with His Father.

Let us give glory to Jesus and the Father for this great moment in history. Yes, let us offer continual thanksgiving and praise for He is Wonderful. Hallelujah and all glory to the Lamb.

This ends our look into Psalm eighteen and the secrets it reveals of the moments after Jesus cried about being forsaken. From this Psalm, we see the finished work of the cross. We also know, for certain, that the Father and Jesus were united never to be separated again.

We know the work is finished. We know the price is paid. We also should know we need to carry the cross and let it finish its work in us. Let us give all glory to God and the Lamb! The victory of this moment and the victory in our lives only will come from the power of God in the cross. It is even as I Corinthians 1:18 says. The preaching of the cross is the power of God. Hallelujah to the Lamb of God!

All eternity waited for that moment when the Lamb's spirit broke from that one blow. Heaven's hush could be heard as Jesus' Spirit broke and He made that awesome cry. All heaven's inhabitants looked to the darkness, the dwelling place of God, to see what our heavenly Father would do. Psalm 18 tells us just what He did.

Having the understanding of this book can give you greater wisdom and strength in Christ if you press to be crucified with Him and thus be healed by His bruise. You will forever bow your heart and spirit to Him for your healing. Of great importance, for this knowledge, you can fellowship with Christ's greatest sufferings remembering how He healed you by His bruise.

All will bow before Jesus in the Day of Judgment as His great power and awesomeness is seen. However, we have the wonderful privilege of bowing before Him for His love in suffering so great a sacrifice for us now. We have the awesome opportunity to fellowship with the Lamb over the sufferings of the cross by letting His bruise bring us our healing. We have the opportunity to fellowship with the Lamb in His sufferings by telling of the bruise that brought our healing to others. The first step in this is to let that bruise heal us.

CHAPTER SIXTEEN

"BY HIS BRUISE WE ARE HEALED"

In the literal Greek of the Nestle and Marshall's text, I Peter 2:24 says, "Who the sins of us Himself carried up in the body of Him onto the tree, in order that to sins dying to righteousness we might live; of whom by the bruise you were cured." In the George Berry text, the literal Greek says, "Who our sins Himself bore in His body on the tree, that to sins [we] being dead, to righteousness we may live; by whose bruise ye were healed." The bruise laid upon Jesus on the cross healed us. It cured us. In these words do we find the way our heavenly Father and Jesus looked at sin at the time of the cross. It is so then and today as to how He looks at it. God looks at sin as a disease. He looks at sin the way we look at a disease.

When a flu virus catches us, we must be healed. According to the way we have learned to deal with it, we fight until it is overcome. Our immune system rises up and strikes at it. We take certain herbs to help the immune system or some medicine that reduces the pain of the disease until it can be overcome. Some have and will die from the serious strains of flu for their immune system not being strong enough to fight off the virus. The disease killed them.

The doctor found cancer. We choose natural methods or cutting, chemicals, radiation, and drugs. We win or the cancer wins. If the cancer wins for the immune system to be too weak or the treatments of medicine unable to overcome the disease, then all that is left is to dull the senses so the patient can die in the least amount of pain. If the dreaded disease of cancer captures a body, the different ways of fighting it is not the issue here. The issue is that we must have this cancer removed.

If the heart becomes diseased and nothing can be done, the body soon will die. All the doctors can do is lesson the pain. Just so is it when we are sick, even heartsick for sin's dominance because we would fail to apply the power of the bruise of Christ to heal us.

Most of our soul doctors try to lessen the pain. By saying things that ease the conscience but fail to remove the sin, they condemn the sinner to spiritual and possibly eternal death. As I have said before, James tells us sin, when it is finished, brings forth death. The Apostle Paul warned all, the anesthesia, the painkilling drug of worldly sorrow produces death. That is, it finalizes and locks in the death sin brought forth. Jesus is not such a poor doctor of the soul as those who marginalize sin like drugs lesson the pain of some disease. Beloved, sin is a disease that produces death, a death of separation from God. No, Jesus will never make the disease of sin that destroys the sinning Christian's life a marginal issue. He would attack sin and destroy its power to ever make us sick again if we would just have the faith to let Him.

I tell you the truth; our Lord Jesus and our heavenly Father have the medicine to cure us of all the power of the disease of sin. Will we take it is the question?

The needed medicine of the bruise of Christ not only will remove the effects of the disease, but the cause as well. Yet, we might wonder how doctors of divinity, how many practitioners of spiritual things rather choose some other medicine than the bruise of Christ. Miserable doctors! For Christian doctors to fail to treat sin as a curable disease, the saints listening to them will face the rest of their lives without the cure. Brethren, this should not be so. Jesus' bruise on the cross is there to cure the disease and its cause. We need not die from sin. We need not have it in control of any part of our lives ever again.

Our heavenly Father looks at sin as a disease. Thus, He sent Jesus to become the cure. Jesus' work on the cross brought our healing. It is in the blow He took that bruised Him so deeply that He would cry out to our heavenly Father of being forsaken. Thus, beloved, you will never be forsaken no matter how sick you become. Jesus took our sin and death. He took the death of being forsaken by our heavenly Father so that we would never need even to taste it. Jesus will never leave you though we can leave Him by choosing the disease over the cure (I John 5:16).

God loves us so much that He would see us forever healed rather than controlled by the disease of sin that produces death. The God of all looked at us with so much compassion for our disease that He sent Jesus to the cross to become our cure. Will we take the cure is the question?

Jesus sees sin as a disease as well. All in the world were sick, dying, or dead. He came to give His life for ours. He came to cure us. How else could Jesus fellowship so closely with the worst of sinners of His time? He could eat with them, cleanse them with His words, and be ridiculed by the self-righteous religion of the hour. Let us note that Jesus knew them who were already dead from the disease of the sin nature. He called the religious order of the day, them who had no compassion for the sick, vipers, serpents, and sons of Satan. Jesus poured out compassion and healing to all that were maimed or sick in the natural, who were possessed of devils, and even to some that had died. Like in an allegory, even a parable, Jesus' labor when He was here as a mere man shadowed the great healing He would bring by His work of the cross. Jesus viewed our sin as a curable disease. Otherwise, He never would have gone to the cross to take the bruise that would heal us. How do you view sin?

Will we now have compassion on Jesus? His great love for us brought Him to suffer the most terrible of deaths. Will we now see His love on the cross looking at us and have such compassion that we will let His bruise heal us? If we see the love of Jesus for us, if we see the love of our heavenly Father in sending Him, we will see God's longing to be one with us. Compassion should drive us to apply the bruise so that it would heal us unto unending fellowship with Jesus and our heavenly Father.

Jesus knows sin, like a disease, will bring the death that will separate us from Him. Thus, He spoke of sin as a disease. In three of the four gospels, we see Him relating to sin as a disease. He said, "They that are whole need not a physician; but they that are sick. I came not to call the righteous, but sinners to repentance." Jesus is our Great Physician. In the world, a physician who cannot heal his patients will not have any. They all will die. This kind of testimony will fail to bring new patients to such a doctor. How long must the world look on at our sins and think, "I may be sick, but I am not as sick as those Christians? I do not need their doctor." Brethren, it is time to let the bruise of Christ completely heal us of sin and its effects. Our testimony to the world depends upon it.

The Holy Spirit deals with our sin as a disease as well. Who is it that has not felt the most powerful, even crippling conviction of the Holy Spirit? Like the paralyzing symptoms and effects of some terrible disease warn us of our need to be healed, so does the Holy Spirit's conviction come to warn us of our need for the healing medicine of Christ's bruise on the cross. The Holy Spirit has come to convict the world of sin. He has come to tell just how sick one is. Like a great fever, he warns us of just how sick we are. Who will pay attention to His warnings and who will take the pain killing doctrines of them who believe in being sick more than Jesus' bruise's power to heal?

God's Holy Spirit works through the conscience. It is like our nervous system. When our natural nervous system works properly, we know the symptoms of some disease and can deal with it accordingly. Just so does a good conscience work. The disease of sin takes hold. The Holy Spirit convicts us sending the warning of the result of that disease throughout our entire being. We then will do one of two things. We will respond to the conviction and take the medicine of Christ's bruise in Godly sorrow or we will drug ourselves with the worldly sorrow of much of the present Christian world view of sin.

The doctors and practitioners of Christianity tell us we ever will be under the dominion of sin. They say no one can be free of sin's dominance. One even said, "The Bible expects you to sin." Such drugs as these kill the nervous system of our conscience. It removes the nerves ability to connect to the brain of the Holy Spirit. No longer will the Holy Spirit be able to send God's grief and sorrow into us over our sins. Death to God will cover us.

When conviction comes, The Holy Spirit is seeing our heavenly Father's grief and concern over our entering the disease of sin. The Holy Spirit's conviction for sin is His putting into us the grief of our heavenly Father and our Savior Jesus Christ over our sins. Then, if we receive God's sorrow, we can become one with God's feelings about sin. We will have Godly sorrow. We will know God's sorrow for sin in us. If we unite to the conviction, even God's sorrow, then we cry out, even travail for healing. We will look to Christ's bruise on the cross. It is the medicine of forgiveness, cleansing, and complete healing. God would have us take the medicine, the cure of the bruise of Christ. Will we take all of its power to heal us is the question?

When bacteria make us sick, we must take the full amount of the antibiotics the doctor prescribes. Otherwise, we may not kill all the bacteria and their disease will come back. The bacteria also can increase their immunity to our efforts to kill them. Just so is it with Christ's bruise and the cross. One dose when we are born again will not destroy the sin nature and all the diseases it produces. Paul in his Colossian letter points this out very clearly. We must apply the whole cross to the disease of sin and its cause, the sin nature.

The cross, the bruise, and the blood will work together to make us healthy. The bruise heals all the effects of sin. It takes away the death that keeps us from Jesus and our heavenly Father. It makes us whole again so we can have fellowship with God. The cross crucifies the sin nature that would produce more sin, even more diseases of death. Then, only as we walk in Christ's light, even the light of His cross and His bruise, the blood of the Lamb, like our blood would take away the bacteria, washes away all sin (I John 1:7). It washes away our past sins, our crucified sin nature, and anything the world or Satan would suggest. Who can tell of the joy and peace of living a life healed and kept by the cross, the blood, and the bruise of Christ? The Apostle Paul can. John can. Peter can. Even a multitude of saints that have crucified their flesh with its lusts and passion can according to Galatians 5:24. I pray we can too.

Again, so many doctors and practitioners of today's Christianity tell us the disease is normal. Who in their right mind would say the disease of leprosy, where all the nerves of the body can no longer communicate to the brain, is normal? Yet, this is what I hear from too many doctors of religion.

What doctor of natural medicine would say disease is normal? Therefore, why in the face of plain straight talking scriptures do so many of our spiritual doctors say the disease of sin is normal and being healed not an available option. Why do they ignore Romans 6:14 which says sin shall not have dominion over you? Why do they reject the clear references in Galatians about the overcoming power of the cross? Why do they refuse to believe in the whole healing of the bruise Isaiah wrote of and Peter quoted? Why do they tell us the scriptures of Romans Eight cannot be fulfilled here in the earth when that is where God meant them to be fulfilled? Why do so many practitioners of religion say I John 4:17, which shows we are to become as Jesus is in the earth, cannot happen in the earth? I could go on to a multiplied number of questions like this, but you will find them if you have the faith to believe we can be healed by Christ's bruise. I just want you to know that the Holy Spirit of God looks at sin as needing a cure and convicts us of the need if our conscience's nervous system is healed and thus works properly.

We need to restore the nervous system of our consciences by applying Christ's bruise to it and then stop killing it. Like the old story of the farmer and his watchdog, so have multitudes treated their consciences. The farmer had a big dog tied up in front of his house. One night the dog would not stop barking. Several times the owner would open his window and shout at him to stop his incessant barking, but to no avail. He threw an old shoe at him. The dog barked all the more into the night. Finally, the farmer took his shotgun and killed the dog. For his silencing the watchdog, he now could go to sleep. Then, the thieves that hid in the bushes were able to come and steal all his possessions while the poor farmer slept. The last deed they did was to take the man's life. All this came upon him for not getting up and finding out just what the dog barked about. He could have taken his shotgun and, with the dog, searched out the land unto making the thieves flee. Instead, he silenced the one that was trying to save him. Is not this just how so many would deal with their consciences?

When the Holy Spirit convicts our conscience, it barks out the conviction with all the strength it has. Will we listen or shout for it to be quiet? Will we try to quiet it by throwing the old shoe doctrines of how we all will sin until we die? Finally, will we kill our consciences, even sear it with the hot lead of our shotgun teachings that lets us love the sleep of sin. If we do, the Holy Spirit can no longer awaken us to sin's threat. Satan will be free to steal, kill, and destroy.

What will you believe? The disease of leprosy was a type of the disease of sin in Old Testament. Jesus cured the lepers that came to Him in the natural. He was showing all who have the faith Jesus has in His work on the cross that He would cure any that come to Him with the disease of sin. This is the faith of God. This is the faith of Jesus Christ. Will you have the same faith Jesus and our heavenly Father have in the cross, the bruise, and the blood? Will you have the faith of God?

Can you see it? Jesus not only will take away the symptoms and the results of the disease, but He will heal the cause of sin as well. In our new birth, He will remove our old man, even the old spirit of Adam that loves to sin. He will give us a new spirit, a pure spirit that hates to see the disease of sin ravish our lives.

There is more. Jesus will remove the old heart that responded to the flesh and the sinful carnal nature unto one that He can write His laws of healing, love, and grace. Then, as we continue to press to let the bruise of Christ work, as we continue to carry the cross of Christ with His bruise ever before us as our medicine against the disease of sin, then the sinful nature will soon be crucified. Like Peter, we will say, "By His bruise we were healed." No longer will we call upon the bruise to heal us through forgiveness, restoration, and empowerment. Rather, we will walk in that healing by making the bruise of Christ, our bruise of life. We will have the greatest praise and worship of humbly knowing a life with Jesus without the disease of sin weakening and destroying us. The bruise of Christ will then become the medicine that enhances our immune system against sin.

Yes, the sin nature would be crucified, dead, and buried making us wholly alive to the resurrection life of Christ. Is this not the very gospel the Apostle Paul preached? Who dares preach a different gospel?

You who want this cure of Christ's bruise can have it. You who believe in the power of the cross and the healing power of Christ's bruise can have it. Start by believing and then at every symptom of the disease put it upon the immune system of the cross and Christ's bruise like as taught in Colossians 3:5. Soon enough, like Peter, you will be able to say, "By His bruise, I was healed."

Of the ones who do not believe the bruise of Christ can heal, even make them whole, we might wonder just what they will tell Jesus as the fire judges them. Will they say things like, "The Bible expected us to sin?" Who will dare tell Jesus who will still bear the marks of the nails and spear, "There was no power on earth that could keep us from being dominated by sin?"

We have seen how God looks at sin as curable. How will you look at it? Will you see as so many poor practitioners or will you say with Peter, "By His bruise I was healed?" Will you believe the disease of sin will ever keep you sick? Which is normal in the natural and which should be normal in the spirit?

Let us see sin like God. Let us see it as a disease. It works just like a disease. How many times would you not have done something that the Bible says will keep you out of the kingdom of God, and then could not stop that thing from taking over your whole being? How many times has disease done the same thing to you? Though you fight the disease, you cannot stop it from ravishing your life. How many times have all the diseases of the sin nature taken you where you did not want to go? Like a virus in our blood, we cannot help getting sick. Sin and the sin nature are ruling too many lives that have known Jesus. If we are overrun with sin,

"Sin, when it is finished, brings forth death," even when you do not want to die. It is just like a deadly disease brings death when the one caught by it does not want to die.

God has ordained for us to be healed. Let us see that Christ's bruise can heal us wholly. Then, let us apply the healing balm of our Lord Jesus to the wound that sin has deeply cut into us.

What joy it will be in the first moments of heaven to look into Jesus' eyes and be able to say, "By Your bruise I was healed, even cured of the disease of sin. Yes, Jesus your bruise made me whole." Then, with the 24 elders around the throne, you can shout with them, "Worthy is the Lamb that was slain!" What greater praise can we have?

What sorrow it will be in the first moments of the fires of judgment that we all must face according to the Apostle Paul. We will see the healing Christ's bruise offered us and how we neglected it unto the disease of sin and its effects to dominate our lives in contradiction to Romans 6:14. Truly, Hebrews 2:2-4 will set our doctrines allowing sin ablaze with the most vehement fire. "If the word spoken by angels was steadfast (unalterable), and every transgression and disobedience received a just recompense of reward; how shall we escape, if we neglect so great a salvation; which at the first began to be spoken by the Lord, and was confirmed unto us by them that heard Him; God also bearing them witness, both with signs and wonders, and with divers miracles, and gifts of the Holy Spirit, according to His own will." Let us wonder how shall we escape the fire of judgment if we neglect this great sacrifice of Christ?

When one who is healthy takes to being sick, he obviously knows the difference. The fever, the aches, the pain, the sorrow of weakness, even the feeling of death's door all are obvious compared to being healthy. When one has been spiritually healthy, he or she would know the difference too. If you have been born again by Jesus breathing upon you as seen in John 20:21, you were healthy. You saw the kingdom of God and O what a healthy day that was. Joy, peace, and a right standing with God, all came in the moment Jesus breathed the Holy Spirit upon you (Romans 14:17). Jesus created a new spirit in you. It was a healthy one. Even so, the disease of sin came and it would seem you would fight this sickness the rest of your natural life.

Do you really think this is God's will for us? You know the difference. You want to be healed. God wants you healed by Jesus' bruise. If you apply it to your life everyday, it will bring that healing. Who can desire sin when in fellowship with Jesus' sufferings of the cross? Every day we need to carry the cross and thus apply the bruise of Christ to any sickness that keeps us from fellowshipping with Jesus. The bruise of Christ will ever be before our eyes unto its full healing power working in us. Truly, this is part of carrying the cross. This is part of sharing in Jesus' sufferings. Then, like Peter, we will say, "By His bruise we were healed." Then, we will be healthy. Kingdom peace and joy meant for our lives here in the earth would become ours even when we are compassed by many trials.

Printed in the United States
107758LV00003B/28-75/P